MW00658977

the mermaid mahjong circle

the mermaid mahjong circle

a fairy tale for women

claudia grossman

gatekeeper press
Columbus, Ohio

This book is a work of fiction. The names, characters and events in this book are the products of the author's imagination or are used fictitiously. Any similarity to real persons living or dead is coincidental and not intended by the author.

The Mermaid Mahjong Circle: A Fairy Tale for Women

Published by Gatekeeper Press
2167 Stringtown Rd, Suite 109
Columbus, OH 43123-2989
www.GatekeeperPress.com

Copyright © 2020 by Claudia Grossman
All rights reserved. Neither this book, nor any parts within it may be sold or reproduced in any form or by any electronic or mechanical means, including information storage and retrieval systems without permission in writing from the author. The only exception is by a reviewer, who may quote short excerpts in a review.

The cover design, interior formatting, typesetting, and editorial work for this book are entirely the product of the author. Gatekeeper Press did not participate in and is not responsible for any aspect of these elements.

ISBN (paperback): 9781642379945
eISBN: 9781642379952

To every little girl who ever dreamed of being a mermaid but was afraid of the water … who ever yearned to be a ballerina but was frightened of being onstage … who ever wished she could sing on Broadway but was too shy to make herself heard … let your art be your presence, your strength, your voice.

And to my darling B., who gave me the mirror to see my true self – this is the story I see in my reflection.

* * *

prologue

about mermaids

Some say that mermaids share the same fantastical world as fairies and pixies. According to legend, these elusive, ethereal souls of the sea call to all, but their songs are heard only by those who believe in their magic. But that's just silly. Why would a grown woman believe in mermaids?

about mahjong

Brought to the shores of the United States in the 1920s, mahjong began in China centuries earlier. The classic game of tiles and strategy has a reputation for being a favorite of Jewish grandmothers of past generations and, of course, of Chinese women for even more generations. It enjoys fresh appeal today both as a game and as a social occasion for women of all ages, from 80-year-old grandmas in Hollywood, Florida, to 20-something hipsters in Hollywood, California.

about circles

The beauty of circles is that they go around endlessly, joining people, generations, lifetimes. Sometimes the connection is seamless; sometimes, surprising; and many times, magical.

* * *

chapter 1

lorelei's tale

My name is Lorelei, and my friends tell me that I don't look anywhere near my age of 800 years old. That's encouraging, although there are some days when I feel every bit of those eight centuries pressing down on me.

Before you go off thinking that I'm just a few scales short of a mermaid's tail, I probably should tell you that I'm just that – a mermaid, that is – and that I have, indeed, been around for a long, long time.

Mermaids don't die, and, as long as we wear red while we're on land, we can always return to our home in the sea.

How I came to be is rather a long story. Suffice it to say that to the sea I was born and to the sea I return, time after time. And there's nothing like sea minerals to help keep your skin looking good. Trust me, I know.

Being able to return to the sea whenever I feel the need has proven invaluable. Like that time that Queen Elizabeth (the first one, that is) caught me canoodling with one of her suitors. Before she could order, "Off with her head!" I was off to the seashore, never to appear again in those parts.

Or the time that I inadvertently caused Mrs. O'Leary's cow to kick over that lantern in the barn by tickling her between her ears (the cow, not Mrs. O'Leary). I didn't mean to cause the Chicago Fire – and I disappeared into Lake Michigan before anyone was the wiser.

And who do you think came up with the "two if by sea" part of Paul Revere's historic chant? That was *moi* – although like so much else that is taught in schools today, we mermaids are left out of the telling.

My favorite era, though, has to have been the Renaissance. The men, the paintings, the men, the sculptures, the men, the gorgeous, glorious art, the men ... ah, the men. Whether it was Michelangelo or Titian, Caravaggio or Botticelli (Sandro always had a special place in my heart because of his *Birth of Venus*, a mermaid on the half shell) – the artists who flourished during the Renaissance are my favorites. These days, though, it's women artists who are my work in progress.

I know that you're probably scratching your heard here and thinking that these are just the somewhat scattered musings of your typical 800-year-old.

But they're not.

If there's one thing I've learned in my long, long, *long* life, it's that women need to express themselves. They need to feel beautiful and they need to make beautiful things. Whether it's beautiful children, a beautiful argument in court, a beautiful life-saving gesture, or a beautiful piece of art – women are the nurturers and the creators behind so much of the loveliness in the world.

To that end, I and a few of my dear friends – mermaids who have grown up and old and older still with me – have been on a mission to find a few such special women throughout our lives. Women whose heart is their art and whose art is their heart. Women who are on the verge of creating beauty that resonates. Women who, once they surrender themselves to their artistic calling, will then have the chance to share a fantastical, thrilling few moments of inspiration and magic that will stay with them forever, compliments of my circle of mermaid friends.

This story begins in San Francisco with a single mahjong tile and with two best friends of a certain age named Evie and Hannah. And now, without further ado, once upon a time …

chapter 2

San Francisco, 2017

"It's one of a kind. You won't see that ring on anyone else's hand." Hannah tilted the vintage-style ring so that it caught the light. The rose gold band, designed in a delicate leaf pattern, glowed, while the tiny but brilliant diamonds set among the leaves threw off fairy-light twinkles. She held it out so that her customer could try it on.

"It's stunning," the woman agreed. "And I think it's the perfect birthday gift to give myself." She smiled impishly and handed Hannah her credit card.

"Brava!" Hannah told her. "We all need to celebrate ourselves from time to time."

After wrapping the ring box in the store's signature violet and leaf-green tissue paper, she slipped it into a small white gift bag printed with *Handmade by Hannah*, the name of her shop, and then handed it to her customer.

"Enjoy wearing it," she said warmly. "And happy birthday!"

As the door closed behind her customer, Hannah looked around her shop.

She had designed every piece of jewelry herself, mostly working with yellow, white, or rose gold. She based her designs on patterns she found in nature and often included a sprinkling of gemstones; diamonds, of course, but sometimes amethyst or emerald or ruby. The pieces were uniquely beautiful and sold well.

Hannah had always had a passion for gemstones, ever since she had been a little girl playing with the treasures inside her mother's jewelry box. As a college student majoring in fine arts, she discovered that she could combine her artistic talents with her love of gems, and a passion for jewelry design was born.

Hannah spent her first few years out of college apprenticing to a series of jewelry makers in Europe. Soon after she returned home, her mother, Amanda, the heiress to an enormous publishing empire, passed away suddenly, leaving everything to her only child. Overnight, Hannah was left independently wealthy. She had the freedom not only to open her own shop but also to purchase the precious gems and metals that she needed to make her own jewelry designs a reality. She combined her actual hands-on designing with trips around the world each year to seek new treasures and inspiration. This year, she had been planning to visit China and Japan, in hopes of exploring the world of gems that the Far East offered.

Hannah lived more modestly than her fortune allowed, a trait that she had picked up from her mother, whose friends would have been shocked to know that her mother was a wealthy woman. Hannah owned a beautiful Victorian in Noe Valley – right around the corner from her shop – which she had renovated piece by piece to bring back its original glory. From the brightly colored gingerbread trim to the painstakingly restored wooden floors that glowed with a soft patina, Hannah's home was warm and colorful, a beautifully bohemian nest that wrapped itself around her each day, feeding her creativity and bringing her peace.

Recently, though, she had started feeling a kind of creative restlessness, an urge to do something new. She couldn't yet put her finger on what it was – she found herself having glimpses of it while soaking in the bath each evening, surrounded by the scent of a lighted candle and the soft ocean sounds from a white-noise download on her phone.

Right now, Hannah had to go. After carefully setting the store's alarm and locking up, she took a deep breath of the chilly evening air, pulled a Giants baseball cap down over her silver-blonde curls, and started walking briskly to the Mahjong Wok, where she was meeting Evie for dinner.

chapter 3

It was somewhere between the wonton soup and the kung pao beef that Evie had what she later called her Mermaid Epiphany. Her fortune cookie confirmed it.

"What?" asked Hannah, about to grab a bite of garlic-scented chicken with string beans. Her chopsticks stopped in midair as she waited for an answer.

"What what?"

"What thought just crossed your mind?" Hannah gave in to the amazing aroma and skillfully plucked a piece of chicken and a string bean from her plate and popped them in her mouth. "You know I can always tell when you've just come up with a big idea."

Evie smiled at her longtime friend and attempted to spear a bite of her dinner with chopsticks, but to no avail. Shrugging, she gave up and signaled to the waitress for a fork.

"Not so much an idea but a realization," she said.

"And ...?"

"And I think I'm a mermaid in an alternate life."

Although she tried to maintain a straight face and look supportive, Hannah found that she just couldn't do it. First she giggled, then she guffawed. Then the last sip of jasmine tea she had just swallowed came out her nose.

"Sorry," she sputtered, "but you know that sounds really out there."

"I do," Evie replied.

"And you know you're scared of the water," Hannah added. "You don't even like fish."

"Again, I'm aware of that," Evie said impatiently. "But listen to what happened a couple of days ago."

* * *

Two Days Earlier

"I hear you, I hear you," Evie shouted from her studio at the back of the house, running to shut off the ringing oven timer. She slid across the kitchen floor in her socks, misjudged her speed and the distance, and bumped into the countertop, knocking over the cold cup of tea sitting there. Maisie, her Aussie-mix rescue, had been stretched out near the oven's warmth, but quickly scampered away.

"Sorry, girl," Evie said as she opened the oven door and removed the pan of tuna casserole inside. "Perfect," she said, admiring the crispy brown potato-chip topping and the warm bubbling noodle mixture beneath. Maisie's nose twitched at the enticing aroma. Evie hadn't had tuna casserole since she was a kid because she had grown to dislike fish. But somehow, today, she had a craving. The casserole reminded her of her late mother, who used to make it for Evie's dinner when she got home from her job as a high-school art teacher. The memory made Evie smile.

The casserole safely out of the oven and the teacup safely in the sink, Evie sat down at her kitchen counter and took out the ever-present mini notebook from the pocket of the men's shirt that she wore as a smock. Pulling a drawing pencil out of her hair piled on top of her head, she tried to sketch the essence of the dream she'd had the night before. But it was still hazy, just a cloud of swirling colors with a shaft of light weaving in and out.

Giving up and giving in to temptation, Evie tasted a spoonful of the cooling casserole, covered the rest, and put it into the refrigerator. Then she went back into her studio, attempting yet again to capture her dream on canvas.

Evie had discovered her love for painting as a young girl, and that passion had grown exponentially through the years. After graduating with her degree in fine arts, she had been lucky enough to land a job at a small gallery in the city, owned by a woman named Anne McAllister, a former colleague of one of Evie's art professors. Evie spent a long time learning the business of selling art from Anne, all the while continuing to make her own art. Finally, after having completed a collection of work that she thought was good enough, she let Anne see her paintings. To her shock, Anne offered Evie her own showing at the gallery. It was a huge success. From there, Evie's star took off. Over the next few years, she became financially successful enough to devote herself to painting full-time, selling her work to clients and collectors throughout the city and across the country.

As Evie had told Hannah more than once, she felt that her talent was in her genes. In addition to teaching art, Evie's mother had created beautiful pieces of pottery, glazed in rich jewel tones, as a pastime. Her French grandmother had been a couturier seamstress trained in Paris. To Evie, as it had been to her mother and grandmother, there was absolutely nothing to compare to the joy of creating and working with color.

Evie lived in an airy, bright house in the Marina District of the city. The home, originally owned by her grandmother, Jacquéline, was the house where Evie's mother had grown up. Evie's mother had left it to her, and Evie had turned it into her home and art studio. Big windows flooded her studio with natural light, and her views of the Golden Gate Bridge never failed to make her catch her breath. She and Maisie took long walks through the neighborhood, often passing by the Palace of Fine Arts or strolling along the waterside.

Now, curling into the window seat, sketchpad in hand and Maisie at her feet, Evie closed her eyes, willing last night's dream to come back. Eventually, the outside noise went quiet, and she felt herself relax. She sank more deeply into the seat cushion, and her head fell to the side as she began to doze.

She wasn't sure what woke her, whether it was the cool breeze suddenly blowing through the room or the opalescent beam of light that glimmered through what seemed like clouds of haze. Evie tried to stand up from the window seat but found herself unable to do so. Remarkably, she felt unafraid, watching as the beam flickered peaceably around the room. She felt a mist on her face and flashing movements of bright color passed before her eyes.

"What is this?" she whispered, then reached for her pastels to try to replicate what she was seeing. She quickly drew the beam of light with strokes of blue and rose, sprinkled with scribbles of silver. No sooner had she drawn a few strokes than the beam disappeared, the air went still, and Evie's studio was back to its original state. Looking down at her pad, she saw that it was blank; that her pastels were still in their box; and that her neck had a kink in it from having slept with her head tilted. Maisie chased a rabbit in her own dream, her paws twitching in her sleep.

"Just another weird dream," Evie thought to herself. Until she saw the few drops of luminescent water on the wood floor.

***

"Roof leak?" Hannah asked after listening to Evie's account. "Water-bottle leak? Maisie leak?"

Evie shook her head.

"Well, there's got to be some kind of logical explanation," Hannah insisted, pouring herself another cup of tea. "More?"

"No, thanks," Evie said. "But that's the point – there is no logical explanation for the water on the floor. None." She fiddled with her fortune cookie, spinning it in circles on the tablecloth. "I've been thinking about it, and it kind of feels like I was underwater during the dream, or the vision, or whatever it was. I'm thinking that maybe it was the ocean. And the beam of light was from the sky, like moonlight filtering through. There's only one conclusion."

"And that would be …?" Hannah asked dubiously.

Evie cracked open the cookie and pulled out the slip with her fortune written on it. She read it and gave a little gasp. "I guess I couldn't have said it any better myself," she whispered. She held out the fortune to Hannah.

The mermaid's realm is cool and blue
with silver moonlight shining through.

chapter 4

Saturday dawned a perfect fall morning in San Francisco – sunny and cool with the promise of a warmer afternoon. It was also the perfect morning for tooling around and stopping for a lazy lunch at an outdoor café. Evie picked up Hannah in her Jeep and then headed south out of town toward Half Moon Bay to do just that.

Tom Petty crooned about *Free Falling* as they drove down 19th Avenue and out of the city.

"Any more mermaid dreams?" Hannah asked playfully.

"Go ahead and laugh," Evie said, "but there's something going on here."

"Okay, let's take it logically," Hannah reasoned. "What other evidence is there of your so-called alternative mermaid life?"

Evie turned down the volume of the music. "Well for one thing, all of a sudden I've developed a craving for tuna casserole. And you know I don't like seafood."

"That's it?" Hannah looked skeptical. "Maybe it's just those midlife hormones doing weird things to you."

Evie shook her head. "And the dreams don't feel like dreams. More like I'm suspended in time or under some kind of spell or something." She glanced over quickly at her friend. "I know it sounds ridiculous. But I also know that when I'm there – wherever *there* is – it's strangely familiar. Like I've been there before or … I don't know." She sighed. "Crazy, huh?"

Hannah was silent.

"And there's something else. All of a sudden I feel like something is pushing me to walk on the beach – and you know that's not something I usually do. I'd rather go to a park or a botanical garden. But it's almost like the ocean is calling to me." She looked a little embarrassed. "Or maybe it's just my imagination."

"I don't think so," Hannah said quietly.

"Me either!" Evie said, sounding relieved. "Wait – all of a sudden you're taking my story seriously?"

She pulled into a parking spot along Main Street in Half Moon Bay, and then sat still, looking at her friend intently.

"Evie, remember when we were roommates in college and after a while our cycles seemed to be in sync?"

Evie looked at Hannah strangely. "That was a few decades ago," she answered, "but I remember."

"Well now I think our subconscious selves must be in sync, too," she said. "Because I'm experiencing these ocean 'moments' too. All of a sudden I have this strong desire to make jewelry using gems from the sea, like pearls and coral and aquamarine. What?"

Hannah stopped talking because Evie had a funny look on her face.

"I know that this a minor point in the face of our subconscious intertwining," Evie said. "But legend has it that aquamarines are the favorite jewels of mermaids."

chapter 5

Over lattés and pumpkin cookies (the most delicious pumpkin cookies either of them had ever had, they agreed), Evie and Hannah tried to sort out their new revelations.

"Here's an idea," Evie offered. "Maybe we're going about this the wrong way. Maybe not everything needs a logical explanation. Maybe this is just one of those stars-aligned-in-the-universe, cosmos-unfolding-a-new-layer kind of thing."

Hannah raised her eyebrow skeptically. "Seriously?"

Evie shrugged. "Sort of. Maybe, rather than spending our time trying to figure out the *how*, we should look at the *why*."

Hannah licked the last of the cookie crumbs off her fingertips. "You mean, rather than look for logic, we should look for some kind of less ordinary, more organic truth?"

"Whoa," Evie said, holding up her hand. "You know, I've come to hate it when people use the word 'organic' to describe anything other than chemistry or food. What does it really mean anyway?"

Hannah chuckled. "Point taken," she agreed. She sipped her latté. "Remember that organic chemistry class we took junior year because we were advised that art majors needed to round out their education?"

Evie grinned. "I don't know how we passed."

"We passed?" Hannah looked surprised. "I guess I just blocked that whole semester from memory."

Evie shuddered. "Turns out our education didn't need to be any rounder than it was. And," she changed the subject, "unless we want to get rounder sitting here eating cookies – I saw you eyeing that bakery counter again – let's take a stroll."

"Nice segue," Hannah remarked. Then, "The beach?" she asked.

"Where else?"

When is a walk on the beach not a walk on the beach? When it gets sidetracked by something even more compelling, they would later recall.

As Evie and Hannah began their stroll through the town's streets leading to the beach, they passed an old cottage that looked as if it hadn't been lived in for a while. The paint was peeling off the faded door; one of the two cracked front shutters hung loosely; and the front yard was overgrown with weeds.

"That could be such a cute little house," Hannah commented. "It looks like it just needs a good sprucing up on the outside."

"And who knows what else on the inside?" Evie replied.

The afternoon sun upon them, they picked up their pace until they got to the shoreline. The autumn sun was a gentle glow in the sky, turning the sand a dark gold color where it lay damp and cool against the ongoing kiss of the waves. The two friends took off their shoes as they began their stroll.

Evie took a deep cleansing breath. "It's so peaceful here," she said. "I don't remember ever feeling so relaxed and yet so aware at the same time."

Hannah looked over at her friend fondly. "And you say you'd rather walk in a garden," she teased, but then grew thoughtful. "I think I know what you mean, though. There's some kind of blissed-out, gratitude vibe going on here." She laughed. "Now I'm the one sounding like a flower child." Shaking her head, she ran a few steps ahead, leaving her footprints behind.

Evie chuckled and walked back to where the sand was dry and seductively warm from the sunshine. She sat down and let herself sink into it, burying her toes and feeling utterly content.

She must have dozed off because the next thing she remembered was her toes feeling cold.

"Hey, Mermaid Girl, it's time to wake up. You're just about to get swallowed up by the ocean," Hannah said, seated at her side. Evie opened her eyes and saw that the tide had found her toes and had planted a few tiny shells around them. Hannah scooped up the shells, stood up, and put them in the pocket of her denim jacket while Evie stretched in a salute to the lowering sun.

The women walked back in the direction that they had come, Hannah leading the way. Evie's hair blew loose from the chopstick holding it in a bun and Hannah's curls rippled in the salt air. They were almost to the point where they had first walked onto the beach when Hannah stopped dead in her tracks while Evie, who had been focusing on her newly painted toenails, walked right into her.

Hannah turned around, her previously wind-burned rosy cheeks now without color.

"Hannah, are you okay? You look as if you've seen a ghost," Evie said worriedly. "Here, drink some water." She held out her bottle.

But Hannah only shook her head and opened her hand to show Evie the shells that had been in her pocket. "What is it?" Evie asked.

"Take a look."

Evie sorted through the shells with her fingertip. "Let's see. Sand dollars, some sea glass, a pretty piece of abalone ..." Her voice dropped off.

Lying in Hannah's hand was an ivory charm, oblong in shape. One side bore the carved image of a mermaid, etched in blues and greens, holding a tiny aquamarine. On the other side were a series of dots in bright red and yellow.

"Okay." Hannah was quiet for a moment, thinking. "This mermaid thing certainly looks like more than a coincidence," she conceded. "And this," she said, referring to the charm, "looks like a mahjong tile."

chapter 6

On their walk back toward the Jeep, Evie looked over and noticed the cottage that they had passed earlier – although it had undergone a complete transformation. There was a yard sale taking place in the front yard, which was now covered in broken seashells instead of weeds, and the house now boasted a bright red door and vivid yellow shutters, perfectly in place.

"Hannah, that's the house we saw earlier – the one that was all rundown on the outside, remember? How did it change so quickly? It doesn't make sense," she said, careful to keep her voice down.

"Must have been a different house," Hannah reasoned. "Look at all the cool stuff for sale!" She indicated the trove of vintage clothing and jewelry strewn about on a few card tables. "It looks like the inside of a closet from the 1940s!" Now she took the lead and pulled Evie closer so that they could both take a look.

The first thing that they noticed was a spectacular selection of dresses, all in rich colors and prints, with beautiful buttons, little collars, and big skirts. Piles of dainty gloves, in shades ranging from dove grey to lilac to bluebell to pistachio, were strewn on one table. Purses in velvet, in shiny patent leather, in silk with embroidered designs, and in smooth satin were on the next. Rows of open-toed shoes, some with ankle straps, stood nearby, as if waiting to be stepped into and danced away.

"Oh, my," Evie uttered. "I could wear every piece here and never buy anything new."

Hannah nodded. "I'm with you – everything is just so vintage. And in such perfect condition. I think my mother wore stuff like this when she was a young woman. At least it looks that way in some of the old photos I have of her."

"Mine too," Evie said. "It's as if the women back then all looked like movie stars just by getting dressed each morning."

"Oooh, look here," Hannah said excitedly. "This jewelry is so much fun." She was running her fingers through piles of mostly costume jewelry – brooches and charm bracelets, Bakelite bangles and earrings, necklaces and cocktail rings – all in a rainbow of colors and shapes from flowers to fruit, butterflies to birds.

"Look at this," Hannah said softly. In her hand was a delicate chain from which dangled an oblong-shaped charm encased in silver. The charm was made of aged ivory and etched on one side in blue and green with the faded, although unmistakable, image of a mermaid, her hair flowing around her, her hand holding the tiniest of blue gems. The other side of the charm featured a floral design.

"That charm matches the tile we found on the beach," Evie said softly.

"It looks like a mahjong tile too," said Hannah, puzzled. "The silverwork here is exquisite." Then she frowned. "There's no price written on the tag, although the workmanship alone makes it quite valuable, to say nothing of its age. It looks like it's from the 1920s or so. And see the aquamarine embedded in it? There must be someone here we can ask about its price and its provenance."

Looking around, they suddenly realized that they were the only two customers at the sale. Then Evie saw a flash of movement behind the yellow-shuttered front window and, a moment later, a woman emerged. Her long silvery hair was held back off her lined face by a shell-shaped comb. Her aquamarine eyes sparkled brightly, and her skin glowed like the palest pink pearl. She wore a long, boho-style dress in ruby red that gave the illusion that she was floating across the yard. Despite her advanced age, her step was sure, her stride smooth, her posture impeccable.

"May I help you?" she asked in a soft, mellifluous voice. "Ah, I see you've discovered one of my favorite things." She nodded at the mermaid necklace.

"It's beautiful." Hannah smiled. "And so unusual. May I ask how much you want for it?"

The woman's eyes moved to Evie. "This piece calls to you, doesn't it, dear?" she asked.

Wordlessly, Evie nodded, as if in a trance.

The woman peered at Evie intently. “It’s been waiting for you,” she said softly.

“And the price?” Hannah asked, sensing that the woman was about to drive the price higher because she knew how interested Evie was.

“The necklace is yours,” the woman said to Evie. “It has waited a long time to meet its rightful owner and, finally, you’re here.”

“You mean you’re just giving me the necklace?” Evie asked, floored.

“How can she be the rightful owner?” Hannah asked, equally surprised. “She’s never even seen the necklace before.”

Lorelei waited to answer until she had fastened the chain around Evie’s neck. The tile charm settled into the hollow of her throat comfortably. The woman looked at Evie appraisingly. “Have you been having the dream?” she asked. “Have you seen the moonlight through the water?”

Evie turned pale. How did the old woman know? Evie’s world tilted suddenly and then all went dark.

chapter 7

When Evie opened her eyes, she found herself lying on a soft couch, a cold cloth on her head, with Hannah sitting next to her holding her hand and looking worried.

"What happened?" Evie asked, momentarily confused.

"You had a bit of a shock and just about fainted," Hannah told her. "Lorelei and I managed to get you inside the house. Good thing you didn't have any more pumpkin cookies or I'm not sure we could have lifted you," she joked.

"Lorelei?"

"The woman whose house this is," Hannah explained. "The woman who gave you the mermaid mahjong tile necklace."

At the mention of the necklace, awareness flashed in Evie's eyes and she tried to sit up.

"Take it slow," Hannah cautioned. "You don't want to get dizzy."

At that moment, Lorelei stepped into the room, carrying a tray with steaming cups of tea and a plate of scones.

"How are you feeling?" she asked Evie. "I'm so sorry if I upset you."

"I'm not upset," Evie said, "I think I'm a little bit freaked out. Or maybe a lot."

"Here, have some chamomile tea. It will help calm you." Lorelei offered her a cup. "And try a scone. You'll feel better if you eat something."

The three women sipped and nibbled for a few moments before Lorelei sat back and said, "I owe you an explanation, Evie. I didn't mean to shock you earlier, but now that you two are finally here and part of the circle, I was too excited to hold back."

"Circle?" Hannah asked. "I don't know what you're talking about." Evie looked equally at a loss.

"Have you found yourself inspired by the gems of the sea?" Lorelei asked Hannah softly. "Have the sounds of the ocean been soothing you as you create new designs?" She peered closely into Hannah's eyes. "Has a mermaid found you, as well?"

It was Hannah's turn to freak out. "What is this?" she asked. "Who are you?" She pulled the mermaid mahjong tile from her pocket with a shaking hand. "I found this on the beach."

"Ah, it's happening more quickly than I thought," Lorelei said, almost to herself. She touched both Hannah and Evie lightly on the arm. "You could say that I'm an artist like the both of you," she said somewhat cryptically. "If you trust me, and trust yourselves, you will soon discover a creative realm unlike anything you've ever experienced," she finished.

"Sounds like an acid trip," Hannah commented dryly.

"I understand your skepticism," Lorelei said. "You'll need to take a leap of faith, but it will be so worth it." She smiled. "I'm neither here to hurt you nor to lead you astray. I give you my word." She looked over at Evie. "Let my gift of the mermaid necklace be a symbol of that promise."

"I don't know," Hannah mused. "This seems like a trick – like those people who claim to be mediums. They con you into believing that they have reached your dearly departed when, in reality, the banging you hear at a séance is being made by one of their cronies hiding downstairs. Or the psychics who swear that they can tell your future just by reading your palm, but the stuff they tell you is really kind of generic."

"I understand," Lorelei answered. "But think about it, Hannah. You discovered the mermaid tile on the beach. You and Evie came to my yard sale; you picked out the piece of jewelry. That had nothing to do with me. I already knew about you both – I knew that Evie has been having strange dreams. That you have been thinking of visiting Asia, learning about pearls and coral and aquamarine, and hoping to design a new line of jewelry based on the sea. I've been watching for both of you now for a long time."

"But how could you know …?" Hannah's voice trailed off.

"The circle," Lorelei answered her. Hannah just looked bewildered.

"Do you really know what I've been dreaming about?" Now it was Evie's turn to wonder.

"A beam of light in shades of rose and blue with bits of silver? As if you're at the bottom of the ocean and looking up at the moonlight?"

Evie gasped and Hannah spat out her tea. "I've really got to work on my table manners," she muttered.

"This is way beyond explanation," Evie said. "It's like you were there in my dream with me." She handed Hannah a napkin. "But I'm still not getting the connection."

Lorelei smiled. "Do you ladies play mahjong?" she asked.

chapter 8

"Didn't your mother play mahjong?" Hannah asked Evie, polishing off the last of the scones.

Evie nodded. "Every week my mother and three of her friends would get together to play, usually at our house," she remembered.

Hannah smiled. "My mother, too. I remember coming home after school and the ladies would be sitting around a card table, a pile of mahjong tiles between them, and cake and coffee ready for when they took a break. That was a long time ago."

Lorelei watched her two young guests delightedly. "So you're familiar with the game," she said. "But have you ever played?"

Both Evie and Hannah shook their heads.

"It's timeless, actually. And it has a true romance behind it – particularly the story of one very special mahjong set. Once you hear it, you'll better understand everything that's happened."

"Would that mahjong set be connected to the tile in the necklace and the one on the beach?" Evie was almost afraid to ask.

"Listen to the story," Lorelei invited them.

She opened a window to let in a salty breeze and the soothing sound of the waves. Evie curled up under a soft jade-colored afghan while Hannah snuggled comfortably against an overstuffed raspberry silk pillow, as Lorelei's voice transported them to another time and place.

chapter 9

Shanghai, Winter 1921

"It has to be perfect," William St. John had told the craftsman. "Each tile must be a work of art."

Li Jun had nodded in understanding. His customer, an American businessman, had been clear in what he wanted – the finest mahjong set that Li Jun could create. Money was no object, William had explained through an interpreter. The craftsman was to use the finest ivory in making the tiles, and each tile was to be etched by hand using the most brilliant of inks. The set was meant as a very special kind of gift for his wife, Ella – a birthday present for the love of his life.

Ella St. John was a beautiful woman, with sea-green eyes and strawberry-blonde hair that she wore in an elegant chignon. She and William had married a decade earlier, and William knew that he had found the love of his life. The couple's only child, a little girl named Pearl, was a tiny version of her mother, but with aquamarine eyes and with platinum hair that her mother braided each morning. Although she was delicate, the six-year-old let nothing stop her, and she loved the adventure of sailing to China with her parents. Each evening Ella would put her to bed with stories about mermaids – particularly Hans Christian Andersen's The Little Mermaid. *The wonderful stories sent Pearl off to dreamland with stars in her eyes. Oftentimes after her mother had left the nursery, Pearl would wake up from one of her mermaid dreams to see a real mermaid watching over her. The mermaid would always kiss Pearl on the forehead and then disappear, leaving behind just a few drops of luminescent water on the nursery floor.*

It was hard to tell who loved the mermaids more, Ella or Pearl, but mother and daughter were both enchanted with the creatures. And Pearl claimed more than once that she wanted to grow up to be a mermaid.

While William tended to his business affairs, Ella would take Pearl for daily strolls through Shanghai. On one such stroll through a lovely park, she noticed a group of men playing a fascinating game with tiles. Pearl was entranced by the rhythmic clicking of the tiles and watched, wide-eyed, alongside her mother. Such was Ella's introduction to mahjong.

William encouraged Ella to learn the game and arranged for a local woman to teach it to her. Precocious for her age, Pearl would sit in on the lessons, even if it was just for a chance to play with handfuls of the tiles between games.

It had been nearly a year since William had commissioned Li Jun for the mahjong set so that Ella would be able to take it with her when they returned home to the States. Their ship was sailing in a few weeks, and William was eager to finally see the set and give it to his wife.

When Li Jun had asked him a year earlier if there was any special kind of design he wanted on the mahjong tiles, William had answered immediately. "Mermaids," he said. "Beautiful, happy mermaids." He handed Li Jun a velvet pouch. "And these," he added.

And now, the mahjong set was finally ready. William couldn't wait to see Ella's expression when she saw it – but no one could have imagined how powerful those tiles would be.

chapter 10

Evie and Hannah sat there utterly still, their eyes wide.

"And what?" Hannah whispered. "What was in the pouch?"

Lorelei gave a small smile. "That's enough storytelling for today," she said briskly.

"But we need to know how the story turns out," Evie pleaded. "You have to tell us what happened to Ella and William and the mahjong set!"

Lorelei laughed lightly but stood firm. "The entire story will be revealed when the time is right. If you let it," she told them. "In the meantime, trust in your hearts and trust in the signs that the universe will send you."

"But –" Hannah tried again.

Lorelei hurried to shut the window as the breeze turned chilly and the sun began to set. "Go now," she said. "Remember to keep your hearts and your minds open to possibility."

Evie and Hannah rose reluctantly and followed Lorelei to the red door of her home. Lorelei hugged them each briefly. Then the door clicked shut behind them.

"I'm without speech," Evie said, turning to her good friend as they headed in the direction of the Jeep. "What was all that? Who was that woman? Are we in an alternate universe? Am I hallucinating?"

"So much for your being speechless." Hannah observed. "And the answers are 'I don't know,' 'I don't know,' 'I'm not sure,' and 'If you are, so am I.'"

Evie shook her head. "Maybe we need to just let this whole experience be what it is," she said.

"Oh, God, again with the hippie-meets-free-spirit-meets-moon-child talk?" Hannah looked exasperated. "What is it exactly that you're saying?"

"Arguing on the side of reason, maybe this is just a big hoax. Maybe we're being punked," said Evie, "although I don't imagine Lorelei knows what that even is. And there's no way someone could intrude on our dreams and inspirations. So why don't we just let it play out? I mean, we've both been around long enough to know that not everything in life has a perfectly logical explanation. Maybe this is our chance to experience something…" she paused for words, "something just a little bit mystical."

"Evie, I don't think –" Hannah began dubiously.

"Oh, come on," Evie interrupted. "What have we got to lose? Maybe there is another realm out there. Maybe, for some strange reason, we get to see it. And maybe, just maybe, if we go along, we'll experience something completely life-changing."

"Sort of like a suspension of disbelief," Hannah mused.

"Exactly." Evie smiled at her friend. "Let's just suspend our disbelief and let this adventure take us where it will."

Hannah nodded. "Okay," she agreed, a little reluctantly. "But maybe we're just two post-menopausal babes who are losing their minds just a little."

Evie giggled. "There's always that," she said.

chapter 11

It was about two weeks later before Evie and Hannah had the chance to get together again.

Evie had been busy trying to finish a new series of paintings for a show that her agent had gotten her at a gallery near Union Square. She had only one more piece to complete – the painting based on her recent undersea dream. Or so she thought.

At the same time, Hannah had immersed herself in her new jewelry line – Ocean's Enchantment, she was thinking of calling it – and was literally up to her elbows in sketches. It was as if a light had been turned on in her imagination, and the ideas for rings and bracelets, brooches and earrings, poured out of her. Earrings of gorgeous gray Tahitian pearls set into silver, brooches carved of angel skin coral in the shape of koi, rose gold charms shaped as oyster shells, each one bearing a beautiful, creamy pearl. And her favorite design so far – a pair of teardrop-shaped aquamarine earrings set into platinum that she named Mermaid's Tears. She scheduled her buyer to visit the Far East and Australia over the next several weeks and gave her detailed instructions as to what kind of gems she was seeking.

It was a cold, drizzly evening when they finally grabbed some dinner. Both women thought that a bowl of hot soup – won ton for Evie, hot and sour for Hannah – sounded perfect. Hannah was already seated in a booth when Evie dashed into the Mahjong Wok.

"Sorry I'm late," she said, sounding a little breathless. "I kind of lost track of time."

"Not a problem." Hannah knew that her friend could get lost in her work for hours. "I've ordered us soup and a pot of tea."

Evie shrugged out of her coat. "Great," she said. "Thanks." She unwound a deep blue scarf from around her neck and Hannah gasped in surprise as she noticed the mermaid necklace. Evie saw Hannah's expression and smiled. "I've taken to wearing it," she explained. "I know this sounds silly, but when I've got it on I feel … I don't know … more powerful creatively. It's like a muse to me."

"Nothing silly about that," Hannah replied. "All the greats had their muses. Of course, in most cases, the muses were real people. But whatever works for you."

Evie smiled across the table at Hannah just as their waitress arrived carrying a tray loaded with a teapot, teacups, and the bowls of soup. She was a young woman with black hair held back in a ponytail and almond-shaped eyes that were an unusual shade of dark blue-green. "Here you go, ladies," she said setting everything down on the table. "My name is Julie, and I'll come back in a few minutes to take your dinner order." She smiled at Hannah, but, when she turned toward Evie, she froze, just staring. Then she spun around on her heel and quickly headed back to the kitchen.

"What was that all about?" Hannah asked quizzically.

"Beats me." Evie shrugged. "Let's decide what we want to eat. All this creativity makes me hungry."

They made small talk as they ate their soup and looked over the menu. "I'm going to try the moo shu pork," Hannah told Julie when she returned. "I'll go with the beef lo mein," Evie said.

"May I recommend the shrimp in lobster sauce?" Julie asked them.

Evie looked puzzled. "No, thank you," she said politely. "I'd like the lo mein."

"Are you sure? The shrimp comes very highly recommended – for both of you," Julie insisted nervously.

"Is there a problem –" Hannah began, but Evie touched her arm.

She looked at Julie steadily, then nodded. "I think we will have the shrimp in lobster sauce," she said. The waitress, a look of relief on her face, took their menus and then rushed away.

"Why are you ordering the shrimp for us?" Hannah demanded. "Number one, you don't even like seafood and, number two, I'm in a moo shu mood."

"I'm not sure," Evie admitted, "but when she said it was recommended for us, all of a sudden I had a strange craving for it. It feels like someone is sending us a sign."

"Feels like someone is working on a reduced tip, if you ask me," Hannah said, sounding irritated.

This time, when Julie returned to the table, she was accompanied by an elderly Chinese woman dressed in a deep red cheongsam, her long white hair in a single braid, and her eyes the same unusual dark blue-green. "This is my great-grandmother, Hai Ling," Julie said as she set down their plates carefully. The older woman motioned for them to eat.

Hannah tried the shrimp and immediately said, "This is amazing."

Evie took one bite and fell in love. "This is so unbelievably delicious," she practically moaned. "I can't believe I've never tried it before."

The old woman looked at her appraisingly. "You've never tried it because you weren't ready for it. Until now." Evie stopped eating, her fork midair; Hannah dropped her chopsticks outright.

"Those are the same words we heard from Lorelei." Evie looked dumbfounded.

"Ah, Lorelei," the old woman said, smiling. "Dear Lorelei. She was right about the two of you."

"Right about us?" Evie asked. "What exactly did she tell you?"

"You know Lorelei?" Hannah asked, incredulous.

"We've known each other for a very long time," the woman responded to Hannah. "And to answer your question, Evie, Lorelei was right about how your time for learning the full story is almost here."

"The full story? You mean the story about the mermaid mahjong set?" Instinctively Evie felt for the charm dangling from her neck.

The woman nodded.

"You know about the mahjong set?" Hannah asked excitedly.

"Of course I do." Hai Ling laughed. "My grandfather was Li Jun." At their looks of disbelief, she added, "My grandmother was his model for the mermaid."

chapter 12

Evie's and Hannah's mouths dropped open.

"You mean ..." Evie's voice fell off. She couldn't finish her sentence.

"I can't even," Hannah said, shaking her head. "How is this all possible?"

Hai Ling fiddled with the neckline of her cheongsam and pulled out a thin red ribbon with a charm on it that seemed to match Evie's. "My grandparents raised me," she told them. "When I was little, I would spend hours in my grandfather's workshop while he carved mahjong sets and pieces of decorative art for his customers." She got a faraway look in her eyes. "The mermaid set was very special to him because my grandmother was his muse for it; I loved it because of her likeness on the tiles. I believed that she was a mermaid."

Evie and Hannah hung onto every word, barely breathing.

"My grandfather carved a tile for me as a gift. He wrapped it in silver, and my grandmother put it on a red ribbon so that I could wear it wherever I went in life and feel as if my grandparents were always with me." Her eyes teared up.

"So my tile is a copy of yours?" Evie asked.

"Oh, no," said Hai Ling definitively. "Yours is also an original – it is a Flowers tile from the actual set." She motioned to Evie to turn her tile around and pointed out the flower image engraved on its other side. Evie and Hannah stared at her.

"And I found this tile on the beach on the same day that Lorelei gave Evie the necklace," Hannah said, pulling the mahjong tile from her purse.

"That is as it should be," Hai Ling intoned. "Also an original. It would be best, Hannah, if you took that tile and set it into a necklace for yourself."

"I was thinking of doing just that," Hannah said thoughtfully. "Maybe on a gold chain with a pearl on either side."

Hai Ling nodded approvingly. "And wear the mahjong tile necklaces as you go forward with your daily lives," she instructed them both. "You will find that they bear no less than a magical power to transform your existence. And they will allow you to be recognized by others fortunate enough to share the secret."

"A secret?" Evie asked softly. "About what?"

But Hai Ling only smiled as she turned around and headed back to the kitchen.

Julie returned to the table with a fresh pot of tea. "I hope my grandmother didn't intrude on your dinner," she said apologetically as she loaded their used plates back onto her tray. "Sometimes she gets a little, I don't know, lost in a story from her past. Who knows if it's even true? For as long as I can remember, she has always told me that if I ever saw anyone wearing a necklace similar to hers that I must tell her immediately."

"And how many times have you seen such a person?" Hannah asked curiously.

Julie turned to Evie. "You're the first."

"And your grandmother?" Hannah asked, unsure whether she wanted to hear the answer. "How many other people has she seen wearing a mermaid tile necklace?"

Julie shrugged. "She doesn't talk about it," she said. "As I said, who knows if the whole story is even true or if it's just a figment of her imagination?"

"Of course," Evie said, somewhat doubtfully. "But she did sound awfully convincing."

"I know that she believes it," Julie said quietly. "Beyond that, it's hard to say. Is there anything else you'd like this evening?"

"Just the check," Hannah said. "And thank you. It's been an – er – interesting dinner."

"I'm glad you enjoyed it," Julie said, leaving their check on the table. She smiled and walked away.

Hannah lifted the check up, got a strange look on her face, and the dropped it down again as if it were on fire.

"What is it?" Evie asked. "Is the math wrong?"

"I can't tell," Hannah said. "There's no order written on it."

"Then wha –"

"Just a message:

The mermaid's song, her secret smile,
are meant for those who wear the tile.

"Shut up!" Evie exclaimed. "It doesn't say that."

Silently, Hannah held out the check. Evie whistled softly. "Are you kidding me?" she asked incredulously. Then she saw the drops of water glistening on the tablecloth – luminous, shimmering, unmistakably not from a glass of water.

Hannah followed Evie's gaze and shivered although the restaurant was warm.

"Remember our mantra – take a leap of faith," Evie said.

Hannah rubbed her temples. "Right now, I'm ready to take a leap, all right. Into a hot bath. Or a glass of bourbon."

"We need to get out of here – I need some air." Evie stood up quickly and threw on her coat.

"Right behind you," said Hannah, grabbing her phone and her purse.

The wind chimes hanging inside the door tinkled as they left and a pair of dark blue-green eyes peeked around the kitchen door, seeing everything.

chapter 13

hai ling's tale

Oh, these women make me laugh! Evie and Hannah, that is. I love to see the light of wonder in their eyes as they begin to put together their story and the story of the women who preceded them in this grand treasure hunt. For them, the adventure is just beginning. I remember how it began for me.

When I was a little girl, my grandfather, Li Jun, presented me with my own mermaid mahjong tile and promised me that it would be an ongoing link to both him and my grandmother, his model for the exceptional art. Except he didn't realize that my grandmother was more than just a model; in fact, she was an actual mermaid. Only later on would I find out that my childhood imaginings about her were absolutely real.

My grandmother came to my grandfather when he was looking for a bride. She told him that she was the daughter of a poor farmer and his wife – recently deceased – and that she sought work as a house maid.

Her true story was that she had gotten tangled in the nets of a pearl fisherman off the coast of the South China Sea centuries earlier. She had escaped back to the sea many times since then, always returning out of curiosity about those who lived on the land. When she met and married my grandfather, she was centuries older than he could ever imagine but as beautiful as she was at age 20. Her name was Meili, meaning beautiful, and, oh, she was so lovely that she swept him off his feet.

Years after my grandfather gave me the mahjong tile created in Meili's likeness, my grandmother – my *Po Po* – pulled me aside one evening and sat me down to tell me her real story.

My eyes grew wide, and I remember feeling as if it were a fairy tale.

"Never tell your grandfather," she cautioned me. "This story is only between us. It is a woman's tale. Only certain women will hear it and respond – and I believe that you, Hai Ling, are one such young woman."

"But *Po Po*," I said, "how am I meant to respond?"

"When the time is right, you will know," she answered cryptically.

I stood there transfixed, my mouth agape.

"In the meantime, keep the mahjong tile close to you at all times – wear it around your neck on a red ribbon."

I nodded. "Of course, *Po Po*," I said respectfully.

"And follow your heart and your art," she said.

"My art?" Up until then, the only area in which I had ever shown any kind of artistic ability had been in creating beautiful dishes in the kitchen. Whether tiny pink shrimp or garden vegetables, delicate wontons or intricate platters of beef with glistening noodles, tender rice or golden chicken sprinkled with sesame seeds and chilis, cooking had always come naturally to me. And I knew that my grandparents proudly lauded my skills in the kitchen – my culinary art – as they sought a future husband for me.

"To create beautiful food is, indeed, an art," my grandmother told me. "And to feed a family – what is more heartfelt than that?"

I nodded again.

"Never forget, Hai Ling, your art and your heart are one. Once you believe that – truly believe that – a brilliant new world will open for you. But now," she got to her feet and pulled me to mine, "it's time to cook dinner for your grandfather."

chapter 14

Sailing Back to San Francisco, Late Spring 1921

The inside of the red lacquer mahjong case was lined in gold velvet; the tiles in their compartments glowing like gems. The set held 144 spectacular tiles bearing the game's signature symbols – circles, bamboos, characters, dragons, winds, flowers, seasons – as well as spare blank tiles.

As beautiful as the playing sides of the tiles were with their vivid etchings, it was the backs of the tiles that were truly breathtaking. Each featured a mermaid – some seated on rocks combing their hair, others gliding through the ocean, some perched on the back of seahorses, or plucking single pearls from oysters, or surrounded by sprigs of coral.

But there was more. The back of each tile also featured a tiny aquamarine – sometimes set into a mermaid's hand, or her hair, or her tail. These jewels were what had been in the pouch that William had given the maker of the mahjong set. Aquamarines. Favored by mermaids. And the birthstone of their dearest Pearl.

Ella could only stare at the exquisite set in wonder, speechless at her husband's generosity and the efforts that he'd gone to in having the mahjong set crafted for her. Pearl was delighted with the set, too. Thinking it was a game for her, as children are wont to do, she began to remove the tiles from the case and set them in rows on the stateroom's Aubusson rug.

"No, sweetheart," Ella said, taking the tiles from her. "These tiles are for grown-ups only. Once you're older you can play the game with me. But until then, these aren't to be touched. Do you understand?" she asked. Pearl merely pouted in response.

Her mommy might think those tiles weren't meant for her, but they were mermaid tiles, weren't they? And, more than anything, Pearl wanted to be a mermaid when she grew up.

"Pearl Venus St. John, are you listening to me?" Ella asked, a bit of exasperation creeping into her voice.

"Yes, Mommy," Pearl answered sweetly, but behind her back, her fingers were crossed.

chapter 15

It was about three weeks later that Evie and Hannah were window-shopping along Fillmore Street, looking for a bridal-shower gift for Hannah's niece, Emma. Pausing in front of a small shop, Evie pointed out a tiny, handmade purse of raw, light-blue silk finished with shimmering silvery beading.

"It's beautiful," Hannah agreed. "And it can be Emma's 'something blue!'"

They made their way inside, and as Hannah paid for the one-of-a-kind purse, Evie looked around at the new and vintage wedding gowns and exquisite selection of veils. There were veils made of tulle, of chiffon, of organza, and of lace, some pure white and others aged to an antique ivory. The older lace veils particularly pleased Evie's eye, and she looked through them slowly, taking care not to tear the delicate fabric.

One in particular stopped her mid-browse – a floor-length veil, golden-ivory in color, embroidered with strands of silver and palest blue. The effect was one of a moonlit-washed beach. Upon closer look, Evie was startled to see that the designs picked up in the embroidery were not merely random patterns. Rather, the veil was covered with a pattern of mermaids, so artfully done that, at first glance, it seemed to be a more traditional floral design.

Noticing Evie's interest, the store's owner came over to help. She was stylishly dressed in a handwoven silk tunic embroidered in shades of apple red and amethyst, black cigarette-style trousers, and deep red pumps. She introduced herself as Delia Charlton. "Beautiful, isn't it?" she said.

Evie nodded. "What an unusual pattern," she said. "It looks like mermaids."

"Good eye," Delia complimented her. "This veil was created for a wedding that took place around 1910 here in San Francisco. Apparently, the bride was completely enchanted by mermaids."

"Really," Evie replied, trying to keep her voice from quavering. "Was that unusual for the time period?"

Delia shrugged. "I'm not sure how many veils with this particular pattern were created," she said. "The design of the veil – cap-style, floor-length – is indicative of the times. Many women wore this style of veil with flowers at each side of the cap."

"I've seen photos of brides from back then," Evie said. "That style of veil was so romantic."

Delia nodded. "The bride who wore this particular veil chose not to accessorize it with flowers or ribbons, though."

"No?" Evie could feel her hands getting cold, a premonition of what was coming making her heart race.

"No." Delia went on with what she thought was her charming description, not realizing that Evie was growing paler. "She chose to use aquamarines to anchor each side of the veil's cap."

Evie only stared at her.

"Actually, I believe I have the bride's name here somewhere." She walked over to a desk and pulled an old notebook from the drawer. "Here it is," she said, running her finger down a page. "The veil was made for a socialite from Pacific Heights."

Even before she had finished, Evie knew what her next words would be.

"The bride's name was Ella Morgan. She became Mrs. William St. John."

Evie just stared.

"Were you interested in purchasing the veil for a daughter's wedding?" Delia asked innocently.

Evie snapped back to the moment. "No," she said quickly. "Not a daughter. I'm a collector and this veil is a stunning piece of art."

"It is indeed," the owner said. She quoted the price and Evie tried not to gasp. It was an investment, she thought, in her future. And a sign from the universe.

chapter 16

Hannah had gone outside after purchasing the wedding purse, waiting for Evie in a patch of sunshine.

"I'm so excited about this gift for Em –" she began, stopping suddenly when she looked at Evie's face. "What's wrong? And what is that in the hatbox?"

Evie pulled Hannah over to the small bench outside the shop and motioned for her to sit. "It's an antique bridal veil," she said softly, "embroidered with mermaids."

"Really?" Hannah was intrigued.

"There's more," Evie went on. "It was made for one Ella Morgan."

Hannah just looked at her, puzzled.

"Ella Morgan," said Evie, "who became Ella St. John."

"Oh. My. God." Hannah was stunned. "And you bought it?"

"I thought it would be a key to unraveling our situation," Evie explained. "Even though it probably cost more than a small wedding." She smiled wryly. "I'll show it to you when you come by next time. It really is exquisite."

"Wow." Hannah was quiet, trying to figure something out. "So Ella St. John was interested in mermaids well before Pearl was born. That means that Pearl's passion came from her mother's," she reasoned.

"It would seem."

"So that means that in ordering the mahjong set, William St. John knew of his wife's interest in mermaids," Hannah went on, trying to piece together the story that they had been told by Lorelei with this new information that they had gained from Delia and from the veil itself.

"Not necessarily," Evie said slowly. "The mermaid design on the veil is very subtle. You have to look very closely to see it. Maybe William didn't see it. Maybe he thought that Pearl loved mermaids because of the stories that Ella had read to her. Maybe he had no idea at all that it was his wife who had the real passion to begin with."

"Oh, boy." Hannah sighed. "The mystery continues."

Evie rolled her eyes. "On a lighter note, let's see the purse you bought."

Hannah carefully unwrapped the purse from layers of tissue paper to show Evie. They ooohed and ahhhed over its delicate design. Evie gently opened the frog closure to reveal the inside of the bag, covered in the palest green silk.

"Just gorgeous," she said. Then, "What's this?" She pulled a rolled piece of paper from a tiny hidden pocket. Unrolling it carefully, she smoothed it out before reading the faded handwriting on it.

Something old, something blue,
A veil of secrets parts for you.

"What in the world?" They looked at each other, stunned.

Just then Delia Charlton poked her head outside the door of the shop. "Oh, good, I've caught you," she said, not noticing that Evie and Hannah both looked as if they'd seen a ghost. "I just wanted to let you know that the bridal purse you chose belonged to the same bride as the veil. They were both used by Ella Morgan at her wedding."

Evie's jaw dropped and Hannah just stared.

"In looking through my files about the provenance of both pieces, I've discovered that they were both made by the same person. A woman named Angélique Roland, who was Ella Morgan's private seamstress."

Evie dropped the hatbox holding the veil. "Angélique Roland?" she whispered, barely able to speak. "She was my great-grandmother."

"Really!" Delia Charlton said, seeming pleased. "Talk about coincidence! Or destiny. This veil was obviously waiting for you, its rightful owner."

Evie and Hannah both jumped, startled that Delia had used practically the same words as Lorelei had when the older woman talked about the mahjong tile necklace.

On a hunch, Hannah pulled her own necklace out from under her sweater. She motioned to Evie to do the same.

Delia had turned around briefly to look inside the store. When she turned back, the first things that she noticed were the mahjong tile charms. Her eyes widened slightly and she nodded comprehendingly.

"At last," she said. "The circle becomes larger." Hannah looked mystified; Evie looked slightly queasy.

"We found this note in the purse," Hannah said, showing Delia the small piece of paper.

Delia nodded, unsurprised. She disappeared back into the shop and reappeared a few moments later. "You'll need these," she said, handing them each a small package wrapped in old newspaper.

"What's inside?" Hannah asked eagerly as Evie tried to collect herself.

"Don't open them until you're told," Delia instructed them. "Just go on with your lives and your art. Answers will come to you in time."

"Answers to what?" Hannah began, but Delia just shook her head. From under her tunic, she pulled out a rose-gold chain with a mahjong-tile charm hanging from its center.

Both women just stared at her.

"Don't be afraid," Delia told them. "Just watch and wait."

The two women nodded mutely.

"And say 'hello' to Lorelei and Hai Ling when you see them again."

She went back inside and shut the shop's door, the wind chimes tinkling and twinkling in the afternoon light.

chapter 17

"Let's take all this one thing at a time," Evie said to Hannah as they sat in Evie's kitchen drinking tea afterward.

"You mean let's break down the Twilight Zone into tiny little segments?" Hannah responded sarcastically.

"Seriously," Evie went on. "I feel like we need to take a deep breath and sort through everything. This whole situation started when we found the first mahjong-tile necklace on the beach. Then we stopped at Lorelei's house and found the second one."

"Don't forget that her house was unlived in and rundown when we first passed it, on the way to the beach," Hannah added. "And then it had transformed mysteriously into a charming, fairy-tale cottage by the time we walked back again. How could that have happened?"

Evie nodded. "It just occurred to me, Han," she said slowly. "Maybe the reason for Lorelei's so-called yard sale was to lure us in. We were the only customers. Is it possible that it was visible only to us...?" Her voice trailed off.

"Okay, I'll go with that," Hannah said slowly, "although I can't believe I just said that. All of a sudden I'm accepting this fantastical stuff as fact." She shook her head and continued. "Next, Lorelei told you that you were the rightful owner of a mahjong tile necklace you'd never seen before."

"And then she told us the story about the St. Johns."

"Then there was the strange dinner at the Mahjong Wok with Hai Ling and her necklace."

Hannah stirred another spoonful of sugar into her cup of tea. "Don't even start," she said, noting Evie's look. "I've been trying to cut back but you know I'm a stress eater and sugar is my weakness."

Evie held her hands up. "No judgments." She paused for a second and then went on. "And of course, there are today's revelations."

"I'll take 'Mystical Mermaid Moments for $200,'" Hannah said with a giggle.

"I know how you feel." Evie sighed. "This whole so-called adventure feels overwhelming, unbelievable, enchanting, irresistible, and scary all at once."

"Maybe you should go with 'Adjectives for $400,'" Hannah joked.

"Maybe you should have some more sugar."

The two friends grinned at each other.

"Is it just me or do you feel like we're caught up in a bit of a spiral?" Evie asked thoughtfully, a few minutes later. "I mean, Hai Ling's grandfather carved the mermaid mahjong set and my great-grandmother made Ella St.

John's bridal veil and purse. We met Lorelei who knows Hai Ling and both of them know Delia Charlton – and all three of them own mermaid mahjong tile necklaces. We seem to be drawn to places and things that provide us with mermaid clues and we've heard some of the story about the mahjong set from Lorelei. This whole thing just seems to keep spiraling around itself." She shook her head slowly. "It's enough to make you dizzy."

Hannah suddenly sat up straight. "Spirals are kind of like circles joined together, aren't they?" she asked.

"Okaaay," Evie said slowly, not quite sure where Hannah was going.

"Didn't Lorelei tell us that we're now part of the circle?"

Evie nodded.

"Well, here we are," Hannah said. "Better hold on so that we don't spin off into the great beyond."

chapter 18

Emma's wedding to Charlie was held on a sunny Saturday afternoon in October at the Palace of Fine Arts. Emma, Hannah's only niece and a sculptor, referred to herself as a starving artist. Fortunately, Charlie was an up-and-coming chef at one of the city's new Italian restaurants and had just received rave reviews in the *Chronicle* for his talents. "At least you know you won't go hungry," Hannah had joked to Emma.

Hannah had brought Evie along as her "plus one," and the two friends were looking forward to enjoying their time at the beautiful venue. The ceremony was to take place beneath the palace's famous rotunda, followed by champagne and wedding cake along the colonnade.

"We want a small, simple wedding," Emma had confided in Hannah. "We'd rather put our money toward an amazing honeymoon." And they did, with plans to visit Paris, Florence, and Tuscany.

As Evie and Hannah waited for the ceremony to begin, they looked around the Palace grounds, enchanted as always by the location. The Palace was an architectural jewel, with Grecian-style stone pillars holding up the rotunda and along the colonnade, and arches crafting a beautiful frame against the bright blue sky and rich green lawn. Swans glided by in the lagoon, adding a special touch to the wedding photos.

"What a romantic venue," Evie commented. "This is such a lovely place for a wedding."

Hannah smiled. "Emma and Charlie wanted somewhere that had a special connection to the city," she said. "And Emma has wonderful memories of coming here as a child."

Evie nodded. "It really is a historic part of San Francisco," she said. "Did you know that the Palace of Fine Arts was built as part of the 1915 Panama-Pacific Exposition? The expo was like a world's fair, built partly to celebrate the completion of the Panama Canal and partly to help the city get back on its feet after the 1905 earthquake."

"Go on," Hannah said, interested.

"The exposition ran from February through December 1915. It included multiple palaces, or pavilions, each tied to a different discipline – the Minerals Palace, the Manufacturing Palace, the Transportation Palace – with the Palace of Fine Arts arguably the most beautiful. Works from Renaissance artists as well as pieces of modern art were exhibited here."

"Someone's been doing her homework," Hannah said, impressed.

"There was also a pretty spectacular Tower of Jewels, right up your alley," Evie went on. "It had arches higher than the Arc de Triomphe and was covered with tens of thousands of pieces of colored glass so that it looked as if it were made of jewels dazzling in the light."

"It must have been awesome," Hannah agreed.

"I've always loved the Palace of Fine Arts," Evie commented. "There's something about the 'weeping ladies' carved at the top of the colonnade posts that touches me. The story goes that they are sad at the thought of the loss of art. The idea that this palace was built to keep art alive just gets me every time."

"Wow." Hannah looked at her friend fondly. "You've got the soul of a true artist."

Evie laughed. "Takes one to know one."

At that moment, the wedding began, as Emma entered the rotunda from the colonnade. Her vintage, cream-colored dress flared out from her waist in a tea-length satin skirt with the palest pink lace overlay. She wore a small pillbox hat with a tiny veil atop her shiny pixie-cut hair, wrist-length blush-colored gloves, and 1940s-style, open-toed pumps. She held a dainty bouquet of pale rosebuds. The total effect was enchanting, and the expression on Charlie's face showed that he had fallen under Emma's spell.

So focused on Emma was Evie that she almost missed it. The justice of the peace had just announced Emma and Charlie as husband and wife and they had leaned in for a kiss. At that very moment, at the edge of her peripheral vision, Evie saw what she thought was a swan swim past in the lagoon. It was only later, when she was enjoying a piece of wedding cake, that she realized that swans do not have shimmering tails.

chapter 19

San Francisco, March 1915

It was a night they would never forget. From the moment that Ella and William St. John arrived at the Panama-Pacific Exposition on its opening night, they felt as if they had been transported to some magical place, with sights they had never seen before.

The Tower of Jewels rose nearly 400 feet into the night sky, its walls covered with countless glass gems reflecting colorful brilliance throughout the exposition grounds. So amazing was the display that the stars in the evening sky seemed dim by comparison.

Ella was due to give birth in a month and William had insisted they not go out that evening so that she could stay home and rest. But she was so excited about seeing the exposition – particularly the Palace of Fine Arts – and she had been out so infrequently during her pregnancy that at last he relented,

"As long as you tell me the minute you get tired," he said seriously.

In response, she kissed him on the cheek and went upstairs to get dressed.

They made a handsome couple, he in white tie and tails and she in a dress of iris-blue satin trimmed in matching velvet. In her ears she wore William's latest gift to her – a pair of sapphire, diamond, and aquamarine earrings that brought an added glow to her cheeks.

The moment that they entered the Palace of Fine Arts, Ella was swept up in the exquisiteness of the setting. The palace resembled a Greek temple, with its graceful columns, rich carvings, and impressive rotunda. Lights twinkled on the outdoor lake, where a pair of swans floated by. Paintings by Renaissance masters, many on loan from their museum homes in Europe and others shared by collectors, were carefully hung inside the palace, each one a masterpiece.

Ella took in the pieces by Titian and Caravaggio and Michelangelo, but she was looking for a special painting, one that she and William had admired greatly on their honeymoon five years earlier in Florence.

Suddenly, she grabbed William's arm tightly. "Are you all right, darling?" he asked, concerned. Ella could only nod and point. "Look," she whispered.

And there it was. The Birth of Venus *by Botticelli.*

"There she is," Ella said softly.

"Indeed," William responded. "She's even more beautiful than the first time we saw her."

The painting depicted Venus, the goddess of love, arising from a shell in the sea as she was born into the world. She was surrounded by angels and a woman holding out a red cloth to wrap herself in. Her long blonde hair partially covered her naked body.

"Why, she's a mermaid," Ella said, her eyes wide with recognition. "And she is breathtaking."

"She is," William agreed. "If our baby is a girl, maybe we should name her Venus."

Ella only laughed, but on the way home, as they were driven through the darkened streets, she was lost in thought.

Hours later, Ella woke from a dream of swimming in the sea when she realized that the dampness that she felt was real. Her water had broken, but, before she had a chance to wake William, she was racked by a strong labor pain.

Hearing her moan, William woke immediately. "Is it the baby?" he asked, trying not to sound panicked.

"It can't be," Ella said once the pain had passed and she had caught her breath. "It's too early."

William decided instantly. "Better not to take chances. I'm calling the doctor."

Ella closed her eyes as he ran downstairs to their telephone. "Hush, little one," she said softly, her hands on her abdomen. "You'll be here soon."

Three hours later, Ella and William St. John became parents to a beautiful, healthy baby girl. Ten fingers. Ten toes. A pair of aquamarine eyes. And a million blonde curls. The new mother rested comfortably, certain that the sight of the Birth of Venus had brought about the early birth of Pearl – their gem of the sea.

chapter 20

"Maybe it was the champagne?" Hannah suggested weakly, although she knew that wasn't the case.

Evie shook her head. "Nope, I hadn't had any yet. It was right at the end of the ceremony and I know I saw a mermaid out of the corner of my eye in the lagoon."

The two were strolling through the Ferry Building Marketplace on the Sunday after Emma's wedding, deciding what to have for a late-afternoon lunch.

"Why didn't you tell me yesterday?" Hannah asked.

"I needed to think it through to be sure I wasn't imagining things," Evie said.

In response to Hannah's single raised eyebrow, she went on. "I even had a dream about it," she explained. "And how do you do that with just one eyebrow? Maisie does the same thing."

Hannah shrugged. "Just another of my talents," she said. "What kind of dream?"

Evie was distracted for a moment, looking at the merchants selling everything from freshly baked bread to artisanal cheeses, from exotic cuisines to decadent desserts, from the freshest produce and handmade chocolates, to soups and sandwiches, croissants and cupcakes, and more.

"Evie?"

"Sorry, I'm really hungry and everything looks and smells so good. Let's get our lunch and then I'll tell you all about it."

They spent the next half hour choosing their favorites and then settled at a small table away from the crowd.

"Okay," Hannah said, unwrapping a panini. "Spill."

Evie broke off a piece of baguette and dipped it into her soup. She took a bite and sighed contentedly. "Mmmm, that's good."

"Evie…" Hannah said impatiently.

"I worked on that painting for a couple of hours when I got home," Evie began. "It's beginning to develop a life of its own – almost as if a force outside of my body is directing my paint brush."

Hannah nodded, listening intently. "What does it look like now?"

"It's still sort of abstract," Evie explained. "But it definitely does look like an underwater scene. It's almost like it's blurry, just waiting for me to bring it into focus. There is something new, though. It looks like it's snowing underwater – there's something falling through the ocean from up above."

Evie paused to eat more of her lunch. "I guess the painting was on my mind when I fell asleep because

I dreamed I was in the painting. Something swam by me – I thought it was a fish of some kind. It had this amazing tail that shimmered so brightly, it looked like it was made of jewels. I tried to catch up to it, but it wouldn't let me. It did turn around right before it disappeared, but just as I was about to see it from the front, I woke up."

Hannah had stopped eating in mid-chew when Evie began describing the underwater creature. Caught up in the story, she forgot to hold on to the panini and its filling fell out on the plate.

"Why are we the focus of all this mermaid stuff?" she asked as she attacked the panini with a fork this time.

"You know how scientists believe that all life began in the sea," Evie said thoughtfully. "Well, maybe we're about to discover our family trees – except in our case it's family seaweed."

"You mean you think our ancestors were mermaids?" Hannah was so excited she forgot all about her lunch.

"Shh!" Evie looked around, concerned that someone might be listening in and think that they were a bit crazed. "All I'm saying is that between my great-grandmother's link to Ella St. John and all the mermaid connections and visions we're experiencing, maybe the circle is bigger than we've been thinking. Maybe it goes all the way back to the very beginning."

"Of time?" Hannah asked, wide-eyed.

"Or of legend," Evie said. "I've been doing some research about mermaids recently. Did you know that one of the powers associated with them is their ability to lure men to their doom by hypnotizing them with their song?"

"I've never lured any man anywhere with my singing, that's for sure," Hannah said. "Very nice, these mermaids."

Evie laughed. "It's not all bad," she said. "Actually, it's not mermaids but sirens who are known for sending men to their watery graves with their singing. Remember we read about that in *The Odyssey* in that Classics 101 class we were in freshman year?"

"Vaguely," Hannah said. "I only took that class as a favor to you."

"But mermaids also represent beauty, fertility, and the life-source of the sea. Believers can tell you that they are the underwater versions of ancient goddesses."

"I can do 'goddess' if given the opportunity," Hannah said thoughtfully.

"And you'll really love this part," Evie went on. "Mermaids are supreme accessorizers!"

"Huh?"

"Pearls and aquamarines, mirrors, combs – best-dressed mermaids won't be caught without them!"

"Remember those accessories we saw at Lorelei's yard sale?" Hannah said excitedly. "Do you think it's possible …?" Her voice trailed off.

"For them to have belonged to actual mermaids?" Evie finished for her. "Almost anything is possible, I guess. But where do the mahjong tile necklaces fit in?"

"They're accessories too," Hannah said, thinking aloud.

"True – but what do mermaids and mahjong have in common?"

Hannah suddenly bolted upright. "Not what, but whom," she said.

"Hannah?" Evie leaned in. "What are you talking about?"

"Ella St. John," Hannah whispered. "Think about it, Evie," Hannah went on excitedly. "Ella commissioned your great-grandmother to create that mermaid veil, so she obviously had an interest in mermaids by then."

"Okay."

"But the mermaid pattern on the veil is so subtle that only someone with very sharp eyes would make it out. It's almost like Ella wanted that pattern to be kind of a secret, noticeable only to those looking for it. Remember what the note in the blue bridal purse said – *a veil of secrets parts for you*. Ella's passion for mermaids must be based on something deeper than just a passing fancy."

The two friends grew quiet for a moment.

"Or what if the mermaid pattern in the veil was so subtle because it was my great-grandmother's idea to design it that way? What if Ella's veil was covered with mermaids as a kind of gift or blessing from my great-grandmother, and she wasn't even aware of it until much later?"

Hannah's eyes widened. "Maybe there is some kind of mermaid connection between your great-grandmother and Ella St. John – and maybe that connection is at the root of the mystery. What if you and Ella share a mermaid birthright of some sort?"

"Whoa," Evie said, putting her hands up. "Slow down, cowgirl. You're starting to sound wa-a-a-ay out there."

"From the woman who thought only a few months ago that perhaps she herself was a mermaid."

"Point taken."

Hannah shook her head as if to clear it. "There's definitely something here," she said. "And I say, rather than wait for the big reveal, as Lorelei and Hai Ling and Delia Charlton have all mentioned, we try to figure it out ourselves. We've got a whole lot of clues here. Let's put them all together and try to connect the dots."

"How about a walk to clear our heads?" Evie suggested as they finished their meal. "I know – let's stroll over to see the light installation on the Bay Bridge."

Hannah nodded eagerly. "I've been meaning to do that," she said, "but I haven't had the chance. Great idea!"

The two friends strolled leisurely on the Embarcadero, finding a perfect spot to watch the light show just as dusk slipped into evening.

"It's mesmerizing," Evie said softly, watching as the white lights sparkled and danced along the bridge's vertical cables.

"Did you know that it's considered the world's largest light installation?" Hannah commented. "More lights than even the Eiffel Tower at night!"

"I've read that the installation was only supposed to last for two years, but that fundraising has helped to make it permanent," Evie responded. "Yay, San Francisco!"

"Indeed." Hannah traced the patterns of the lights with her eyes, watching them change from raindrops, to swirls, to ribbons of light that converged and re-formed again and again. And then …

"Wait! Evie – did you see that?"

"What is it?" Evie asked. "What do you see – ohh!"

Captured in the pattern of lights was a pair of mermaid figures, swimming their way across the bridge cables, shimmering in the moonlight. Suddenly, the patterns changed, and a flash of mahjong symbols appeared – first flowers, then bamboos, then dragons and dots. And finally, before either Evie or Hannah could say another word, the image of a mahjong tile glowed in lights as the stars came out.

The two friends looked around, wondering if they were the only ones who had seen the light images. Apparently, they had been, as no one else seemed to recognize anything unusual. When they looked back at the bridge, all they could see was an ongoing masterpiece of light patterns, changing from moment to moment, but revealing neither the mermaids nor the mahjong tile again.

"Everywhere we look it's mermaids," Evie said quietly as they began to stroll away. "Can't you just see those mermaid patterns done up in diamonds?"

Hannah nodded enthusiastically. "I'm already designing in my head," she said. "I'm thinking of an extravagant diamond collar."

"I like that." Evie nodded. Then, "I'm thinking of a mural where the mermaids are done up with touches of gold leaf – yellow, white, and rose gold. Something more than a painting. Maybe a mosaic of some kind?"

"Let's see where we are on all this tomorrow night," Hannah said.

"I'll make the popcorn, you pour the wine," Evie responded. "See you at my place tomorrow."

chapter 21

The next morning, Hannah unlocked the door of her shop and turned on the lights, all the while juggling an iced cappuccino and a lemon bar. The odds of her not dropping or spilling anything were not in her favor.

Congratulating herself for making it to her design table without incident, she sat down and began studying the sketches that she had been working on before the weekend. She couldn't wait to get together with Evie later on and compare creative visions, but there were a few details she needed to work out first.

She tugged absently on the mahjong tile on the chain around her neck as she lost herself in thought. "What if," she thought aloud, "what if I bring the mermaid and the mahjong together?" Grabbing her pencil, her hand moving almost faster than her thoughts, she quickly sketched out a bracelet, unlike any she'd ever created before. The bracelet itself was made of delicate white gold, designed to look like scales. From it were suspended a number of exquisite charms crafted in rich, jewel-colored enamel and touched with a sprinkling of gems. There were four mermaids, each with a different color tail, as well four brilliantly hued mahjong tile charms, each featuring a different pattern of mahjong symbols – dots, flowers, bamboos, and dragons.

Hannah looked at the bracelet sketch for a long time until suddenly, "It's a circle," she said to herself wonderingly. "It all comes together here."

At the same time, Evie was in her studio, lost in thought. Impulsively, she picked up a clean, prepped canvas from a pile against the wall and set it on an easel. Paintbrush in hand, and almost as if an outside force moved it, she swirled multiple rings, each in a different shade of watercolor – blue-green, celadon, sapphire, and deep iris – and each created with multiple brushstrokes. Each ring slightly overlapped the next, forming and filling one large circle, with the visual effect being that of the scales on a mermaid tail. Then, in varying shades of gold and silver, Evie added another layer of delicate images – the small dots, flowers, bamboos, and dragons found on mahjong tiles.

After what seemed like just an instant, Evie took a step back to catch her breath and gain some perspective. And then it hit her.

"It's a circle," she said aloud, wonderingly. "But where does it begin … and where does it end?"

Both Evie and Hannah started talking simultaneously from the moment they got together over wine and popcorn, with Maisie waiting dutifully under the table, hoping for a stray popped kernel to fall into her mouth.

"You go first," Evie said as their words tumbled out over each other.

Hannah took a deep breath. "Okay, here's the deal," she began. "I was sketching out some designs this afternoon and, all of a sudden, this idea came into my mind. I couldn't draw it fast enough – it felt like my hand was outrunning my brain. It's like the idea came to me all at once and I had to put it down on paper before it went away." She pulled her sketches out of her bag and laid them out on the table. "Have a look."

Evie's eyes widened as she took in the drawings of the bracelet. Gently she ran a finger over the figures of the mermaids in brilliant colors joined together by renderings of dainty mahjong tiles. "Hannah, it's breathtaking," she said. "I've never seen anything like it."

"Thanks," Hannah said modestly. "I think that it could be the centerpiece of my Ocean's Enchantment collection."

"I think it's extraordinary," Evie commented.

"What's extraordinary is the flash of creativity that brought it to mind. I've never designed anything like it before," Hannah remarked. "It felt like I was transported to a different plane – my focus was laser sharp." She paused. "Wait a minute," she said excitedly, "do you think this was what Lorelei and Hai Ling and Delia all meant? You know, about how if we let this mermaid magical mystery reveal itself to us, our creative impressions will be heightened?"

Evie just stared at her. Then, "Hang on just a sec," she said and ran to her studio to get the painting she had worked on earlier in the day.

Hannah studied the canvas and then looked at Evie. "It's the same circle," she said incredulously. "We're part of the mahjong mermaids."

Hannah smiled for a moment. "You know, the original mahjong set that belonged to Ella St. John had more than one hundred pieces in it – what do you think happened to the rest of the tiles?"

"I don't know," Evie said slowly. "Why?"

"Because I think that those tiles would be beautiful in our piece," she said. "I mean, what's a mermaid mahjong circle without the mermaid mahjong tiles?"

"Good point." Evie thought a minute. "I know someone who just might have that answer for us."

Hannah looked at her questioningly.

"Ready for another trip to Half Moon Bay?"

chapter 22

"Which one was it?" Hannah asked Evie as they drove through the streets along the beach in Half Moon Bay, Maisie in the backseat, looking for Lorelei's cottage.

"We're looking for either a totally abandoned house with hanging shutters and an overgrown lawn or a fairy-tale kind of cottage with a red door, yellow shutters, and maybe even a yard sale going on," Evie answered, her eyes scouring the streets as she drove along.

But after having crisscrossed the neighborhood numerous times, they were close to giving up.

"I guess it was a figment of our collective imagination," Hannah said gloomily. Then, brightening, "Maybe we should grab some of those pumpkin cookies as a consolation prize."

"Wait! This is the house!" Evie said excitedly, slowing down. "Isn't that front door a faded red? Let's look around."

She, Hannah, and Maisie made their way through the overgrown lawn, the women stepping carefully so as not to trip, Maisie ever graceful on her paws. They were just inches from the door when they heard a rustling behind them. Turning, they saw the sea grasses waving as if in a stiff breeze, although there was none at the time. The fur on Maisie's neck stood straight up and she whimpered. From seemingly nowhere, pages fluttered by, landing at their feet. Then all was still. They picked them up and read.

***

chapter 23

Angélique Roland seemed to be born of the sea. No one knew anything about her birth or her roots in the small French fishing village in which she suddenly appeared; in fact, a story was told that she had been tossed from the sea in a harrowing storm, hid her true identity, and chose to remain on land. The red ribbon that she always wore around her neck, they said, was the magic that allowed her to remain on solid ground.

Over the years, the villagers came to know her as part-girl, part-mermaid; to them, her mother – la mère – was, indeed, la mer, the sea. And Angélique had always let the fantasy stand.

The only time Angélique ever returned to the sea was when she was 17 years old, aboard a ship to America. After making her way to San Francisco, she was lucky enough to find work as a maid in the household of financier James Morgan and his wife, Sarah. Once Sarah saw Angélique's exquisite embroidery and needlework, she offered her a position as her private seamstress.

Sarah Morgan was pregnant when Angélique arrived, her pregnancy a fragile one. She felt ill much of the time and could neither hold down food nor sleep comfortably. Her doctors tried all kinds of treatments with little success. They worried that she would not be able to carry her baby to term. When Angélique offered to help, Sarah weakly agreed.

Angélique fed Sarah potions that she made herself using minerals and healing plants from the sea to help nourish her and her growing baby. And one moonlit night, as the tide turned silver and the stars shone, Sarah gave birth to a beautiful, healthy baby girl whom she named Ella Angela, as a tribute to Angélique. The two women grew close over their shared secret about the sea and its wonders, and the bond between them became unbreakable. From then on, Sarah always thought of her baby daughter as a child of the sea, a mermaid miraculously brought to her by Angélique.

And from the moment that she was old enough to understand, Ella was told the story by her mother. She knew that she had mermaid energy inside of her – and she knew to keep that information as a locked secret in her heart.

chapter 24

"I knew it!" Hannah said the moment they had finished reading the pages. "I knew you had some mermaid blood in you!"

"Wait, wait, wait. Let me process this," Evie said a bit shakily. "We don't know for a fact that Angélique was a mermaid – only that the villagers in her town believed the story about her being found by a fisherman in his net. Maybe she was running away from home and made up the story to keep her family from finding her. Or maybe she just made it up because she didn't want anyone knowing anything about her."

"Or maybe she told it because it was the truth," Hannah finished determinedly.

"All of a sudden you're now believing this kind of fantastical tale?" Evie commented.

"All of a sudden you're painting a mermaid tail," Hannah reminded her. "And all of a sudden the pieces are starting to drop into place. What else do you remember hearing about Angélique?"

"I remember my grandmother, Jacquéline, telling me about her mother, Angélique, being a seamstress and being from France originally before she came to America," Evie responded. "My grandmother, Jacquéline, learned how to do all kinds of needle arts from her before she, herself, went to Paris for some years and trained as a couture seamstress. She passed what she learned down to my mother." She laughed. "Although I'm sad to say that, beyond sewing on a button, my own skills are limited."

"Anything else?"

"I have a vague memory of seeing some sketches that my grandmother showed me of the most beautiful ballgowns that Angélique had designed," Evie said, speaking more rapidly as her memories started to come back. "Angélique's drawing was exquisite – in particular, now that I'm thinking about it, I remember two stunning pieces. One was an evening dress done in iris-colored silk with an empire waist and touches of matching velvet. It was meant as a maternity dress. And if I remember correctly …" she closed her eyes, "… yes, it was labeled *Panama-Pacific Exposition, Opening Night, 1915*."

"Wow."

"And the other sketch was even more beautiful," Evie went on excitedly. "That one was designed in brilliant aquamarine. It had a closely fitted satin top, and a beautiful ballgown skirt done in layers of tulle and scattered with sequins. It was breathtaking."

"Was there any notation on that drawing?" Hannah asked, mesmerized.

Evie nodded. "It said *Anniversary Dinner, Fairmont Hotel, 1926.*"

Hannah nodded, taking it all in.

"Oh, one more thing," Evie said. "Both sketches read, *Designed for Ella St. John.*"

chapter 25

San Francisco, March 1926

"Darling, where are you taking me?" Ella asked William laughingly as he whisked her away one evening.

Dressed to the nines – he in white tails and she in a frothy aquamarine confection of a ballgown – the couple was comfortably ensconced in the backseat of their Rolls Royce Phantom Coupe. The gleaming ebony motorcar made its way through the city streets, affording Ella and William panoramic views of the lights dotting San Francisco Bay and of the hillsides of Marin.

"Oh, nowhere special," William teased her fondly. "I just thought it was a lovely evening for a drive."

"Oh, you!" Ella scolded him playfully. Her hair was pinned back in a simple chignon, enhanced only by a stunning diamond-and-aquamarine brooch in the shape of a star fish, and her eyes sparkled with anticipation.

"Have I told you lately, Mrs. St. John, how desperately and completely in love with you I am?" he asked, holding her hand in his and kissing her on the cheek.

"Me, too, William."

"That's why I wanted us to celebrate this anniversary in a special way," he went on. "The past 15 years have been an incredible gift."

Ella nodded. "I never dreamed I could be so happy," she said softly.

"We, sweetheart, we," he said squeezing her fingers.

Their drive continued downhill and then up again, arriving at the top of Nob Hill and the Grande Dame of San Francisco – the Fairmont Hotel.

As their chauffeur, Brian, opened the door and helped Ella out of the automobile, he smiled at her.

"May I wish you and Mr. St. John the happiest of anniversaries," he said respectfully.

"Why, thank you, Brian," Ella responded. "Thank you so much."

"If you're wondering how Brian knows about our anniversary, it might be because I couldn't keep my excitement to myself," William told her as he led her inside the hotel. "I also told Angélique about it when she was working on your dress. I wanted to make sure that she sewed a little bit of magic into it."

Ella held his arm more tightly in response.

As they entered the marble lobby, Ella couldn't help but gasp. She'd been there many times before with William since the hotel had opened, newly rebuilt after the 1906 earthquake and fires which had all but destroyed it. Those previous visits had been for an evening of dining and dancing. But tonight was different.

Rather than lead her to the hotel's famed dining room, William guided her through a garden at the back of the hotel and up a private elevator.

Ella looked over at William, mystified, but he only offered a mysterious smile.

When they got off the elevator on the eighth floor, they were ushered into the most majestic accommodation that Ella had ever seen or even heard of. It was the extraordinary Penthouse Suite.

Ella was silent with awe as the hotel manager took them on a tour of the suite's three bedrooms, four fireplaces, two-story domed library, billiards room, and full kitchen, where a private chef was putting the finishing touches on their supper. The dining room, enormous enough to hold a seated party for 50, featured a candlelit table for two, intimately placed at a window overlooking the city. Champagne cooled in a silver ice bucket while the table gleamed with cut crystal and silver.

Peonies and tulips, imported for the celebration, graced each room, while a string quartet played Mozart and Vivaldi in the library.

The cost of the suite for even one evening was a king's ransom – but to William St. John, there was no gift too sumptuous for his loving wife.

There was something about her, something so ethereal, that he could neither name nor resist – a loveliness unlike anything he had ever seen or felt from another woman. There was something in her sea-green eyes that enchanted him completely, even after 15 years of marriage. In fact, he was more smitten with her now than ever.

And after midnight, after she had unfastened the brooch that held her long wavy hair and it came tumbling down around her body, after her otherworldly beauty mesmerized him once more, after he made love to her – after all of this, he fell into a deep, contented sleep.

While she, so blissful after their passionate encounter, dreamed of a beautiful place where mermaids swam free.

chapter 26

"But these pages still don't tell us what happened to the rest of the tiles," Evie mused, after telling Hannah about the sketches. The two women remained standing in front of the cottage. "We know about my so-called mermaid ancestry but how do we explain how Lorelei, Hai Ling, Delia Charlton, you, and I all have mahjong tiles from the original set? How did those tiles get from Ella St. John's set into all of our hands?"

There came a tinkle of laughter and the scent of sugar cookies.

"You girls have a lot of questions, don't you?" Lorelei stood before them, framed by the now bright red doorway. "Come in, come in."

Evie and Hannah entered the cottage once again, noting that it looked exactly the same inside as when they had visited weeks earlier. Maisie, needing no invitation, curled up at Lorelei's feet as the older woman seated herself in a seafoam green velvet armchair. Evie and Hannah perched side by side on the overstuffed sofa.

"I do believe it's time to supply you with more of the story," Lorelei began, "although I must say that I'm very impressed with how far you've come."

"Is Evie really a mermaid?" Hannah couldn't help herself.

Lorelei's eyes crinkled up in the corners as she smiled. "That wasn't the question that brought you here," she said, sidestepping the answer. "You wanted to know how the mahjong tiles ended up in your hands and what happened to the rest of them."

"We want to know it all," Hannah insisted.

Lorelei shook her head, her long silvery waves shimmering with the movement. "All in good time," she said firmly. "First things first."

With that, she got up and returned with a platter of freshly baked sugar cookies, a doggie treat for Maisie, and a pot of freshly brewed Earl Grey tea. "Let's go back to little Pearl St. John."

chapter 27

Outside San Francisco Bay, Late Spring 1921

Pearl wanted to listen to her mommy, she really did. But those mermaid mahjong tiles were just too tempting. She knew that they were in the lacquer box that her mommy had put on the top shelf of her closet in their luxurious stateroom. She imagined the mermaids inside longing to escape and return to the ocean where they might swim and play among the starfish and seahorses and dolphins. If she listened very carefully when it was quiet, she thought she could hear them weeping to be freed from their velvet-lined captivity. If only she were big enough to reach up to that top shelf and pull down the box.

It was the day before their ship was scheduled to dock at the harbor in San Francisco that Pearl had her chance. The St. Johns' personal maids had been all aflutter packing up Ella's, William's, and Pearl's wardrobes and belongings. Chaos ensued when one of Ella's afternoon dresses could not be located for hours. It was in that chaos that precocious little Pearl found her opportunity.

All of her mommy's dresses were laid out throughout the cabin, as well as her shoes and purses, furs and jewels, hats and lingerie and more. Included in the vast array was the mahjong set. While the maids ran to and fro, attempting to find the missing dress that Ella had worn to stroll on the deck with William and take afternoon tea (it was eventually located at the back of William's closet where it had been hung by mistake), Pearl managed to pick up the lacquer case and hide it under the thick blanket on her bed.

The next day, when the coast was clear and every maid's attention was turned to finishing the millions of details involved in packing, Pearl managed to slip out the door of the cabin onto the breezy walkway that ran the length of the ship. Ella and William were enjoying breakfast in their private salon; everyone assumed that Pearl was still fast asleep in her bed, dreaming her mermaid dreams.

Once outside the stateroom, Pearl set down the lacquer box at her feet and opened it almost reverently. One by one, she freed each mermaid tile from its place, held it in her hand for a moment, and kissed it gently. Then, "Swim, mermaids, swim back to your home in the sea!" she cried before rising on to her tiptoes and tossing handfuls of the tiles over the railing and into San Francisco Bay.

It was only a few minutes later that William and Ella opened the door of their cabin to enjoy the view of San Francisco coming into sight as the ship sailed close to harbor. The first thing that they saw was Pearl in the midst of the mermaid emancipation, the last two mermaid tiles in her hands.

"Pearl, no!" Ella cried as Pearl flung the final two mermaids into the Bay. William ran forward to pick up their daughter. "Oh, my darling girl, you could have slipped into the ocean!" Ella was practically hysterical with fear at what might have been. William did his best to calm her by putting Pearl into her arms to prove that the little girl was indeed safe.

It wasn't until Ella was assured that Pearl was unhurt that she realized what Pearl had been up to. All of the mahjong mermaid tiles were gone; all that remained was the lacquer box. "Oh, Pearl," she said, "what have you done?"

"The mermaids were crying to get back into the sea, Mommy," Pearl explained. "I had to let them go home – the same way that we're going home."

Ella just looked at her daughter, speechless, caught between anger that Pearl had disobeyed her and thrown away the beautiful, expensive mahjong set, and the much greater feeling of relief that Pearl hadn't fallen overboard herself.

The family went back inside their stateroom, Ella carrying Pearl, and William following, carrying the now-empty box. The little girl looked up at her father, her aquamarine eyes sparkling with happiness at her accomplishment of freeing the mermaids back to the sea. And William couldn't help but wink at her, his precious little mermaid who had him wrapped around her little finger.

chapter 28

"Seriously?" Hannah asked, her mouth agape. "She threw the tiles into the ocean?"

"She did," Lorelei answered. "She set the mermaid tiles free."

"And so some of them sank and some got washed ashore?" Evie asked. "Is that how a few of us found them?"

"Could be," Lorelei said cryptically. "But you have to allow for other forces. Not just the forces of nature."

"What kind of other forces?" Hannah asked, impatient.

Lorelei looked at her appraisingly. "Some might say that you two are forces of nature unto yourselves," she said. "And some might say that there are a lot of forces that control our lives – the forces of fate, of love, of art, of science. You need to find your forces and then you'll find your answers."

"But what about –?" Hannah began, but Lorelei hushed her.

"That's all for now, ladies. Enjoy your cookies and close the door when you leave." Lorelei stood, twirled around, and was gone in a flash. Maisie whimpered.

"I guess that's our cue to leave," Evie said, gathering up Maisie's leash. "Let's go, Hannah."

"Right behind you," Hannah muttered. "No, really – she threw the entire set of tiles into the ocean?!"

chapter 29

the mermaids' tale

The mermaids sat around a small table carved of coral, a pile of mahjong tiles between them. Perched on shells, they regarded the tiles bemusedly. Finally, Lorelei spoke.

"Well, well, well," she said, her voice melodious and clear. "It looks like we've now become pieces of art." She laughed and her companions giggled alongside her.

"My husband crafted these tiles!" Meili exclaimed. "He just finished this set a few weeks ago. He made the tiles for a wealthy American who wanted the mahjong set for his wife." She smiled. "He hated to let these tiles go because he said that each one reminded him of me." She blushed. "I wish that I could tell him that 'his' mermaids have returned to the sea."

"You must never share our secret about being mermaids with any man," Lorelei responded sharply. Then her tone softened. "You know the rules, Meili. We can only let women – certain, gifted women – into our circle."

Meili nodded, her lustrous black hair shimmering in the ocean light. "Of course, Lorelei." Then she brightened. "I do believe my granddaughter, Hai Ling, will be one such woman."

The other mermaids chattered among themselves excitedly at her announcement.

"She is an artist in her own right," Meili went on. "In all my centuries, I've never seen anyone with the kind of kitchen arts that she possesses, even as a young girl." At that, a few passing fish scurried away more quickly, as if fearing becoming a part of one of Hai Ling's artistic plates.

Lorelei nodded. "Perhaps it is time to bring her here to discover our world and her possibilities." She smiled. "But now to the matter at hand – these mahjong tiles."

"Where did they come from?" one of the other mermaids asked, running her fingers through the colorful pile. "How did they end up here?"

"I can answer that." Yet another mermaid, this one with auburn hair and a shimmering amethyst tail responded.

"Yes, Cordelia?"

"Those tiles were thrown into the San Francisco Bay by the daughter of the man who commissioned them from Meili's husband."

A collective mermaid gasp followed.

Cordelia went on. "Lorelei knows the entire story. She was there."

"Oh, please tell it, Lorelei!" The mermaid who had been running her fingers through tiles stopped still. "I can't wait another moment!"

Lorelei smiled and settled in a bit more comfortably on her shell. "I was aboard the ship along with William St. John, his wife, Ella, and their little girl, Pearl, as it sailed from China back to the States." She laughed. "I wanted to see how the other half traveled the ocean.

"I had boarded the ship just before it docked," she went on, "when I heard this huge commotion coming from the upper deck. It seemed that the little girl, Pearl, had believed that these mermaid tiles were real mermaids and wanted to return them to the sea. She disappeared from the family's stateroom and, before they could find her, had thrown all of the tiles into the ocean." She smiled at the memory. "You don't see that happen every day."

At that, one of the other mermaids, this one with titian hair and a tail of glimmering emerald gave a start. "Did you say Ella St. John and her daughter Pearl?" she asked. At Lorelei's nod, she clapped her hands and laughed.

"Are those names familiar to you?" Lorelei asked.

"Of course," the mermaid said. "Ella St. John is my goddaughter. I helped her mother through her pregnancy by using a little bit of sea magic." She smiled.

"I also created Ella's bridal veil." Here, she looked at the circle of mermaids at the table. "The lace had a secret pattern of mermaids woven into it, to remind her of her mermaid connection." She sat thoughtfully for a moment. "It must have worked if little Pearl felt such an affinity for mermaids."

"Angélique, what a beautiful story!" Lorelei said, tears in her eyes. "Maybe when she grows up little Pearl might visit us here." She sat for a moment, lost in thought. "But first, we need to use these tiles for something important."

"Something beautiful," Meili said.

"Something extraordinary," Cordelia added.

Lorelei nodded. "Let the games begin."

chapter 30

After meeting Emma and Charlie for a post-honeymoon breakfast on a Sunday afternoon, Evie and Hannah headed for their favorite nail salon. Over pancakes, Emma had told them about how much she had loved all of the art that they had seen in Florence, while Charlie could not stop raving about the cuisine.

"It's so nice to see them so happy," Evie commented after she and Hannah had chosen their manicure shades. She opted for a low-maintenance pinky-nude while Hannah decided on a shimmery lilac.

"You're right," Hannah agreed. "Emma is absolutely glowing and Charlie looks like he just won the lottery every time he looks at her." She smiled at Evie. "Remember what it was like to be in love like that?" she said dreamily. "You and Danny looked a lot like them 30 years ago."

"I guess it wasn't meant to last," Evie said quietly, thinking about her husband who had died much too young. "But of course I remember." She smiled. "It was lovely." She poked Hannah in the side. "And how many times have you been in love, Hannah?"

"Ever? Or just this year?" Hannah grinned at her friend. "I love men, I really do. Only not enough to share my life with one." She paused. "I guess what I really love is falling in love!"

"Of course you do," Evie said fondly.

Their attention was caught by the salon customer next to them.

"Have you ever been to the 16th Avenue Tiled Steps?" the customer was asking her manicurist. "They're amazing."

"I haven't," the manicurist answered, "but I've heard that they're beautiful."

The woman nodded. "163 steps to the top. But even if you don't climb, if you just look at the stairs from the bottom up, they form the most breathtaking mosaic. And the view from the top is worth every step," she went on. "You can see out to the Golden Gate and beyond."

Evie and Hannah shared a look.

"Think we're up to it?" Hannah asked after the woman had left, her nails painted a bright fire-engine red.

"Let's go," Evie answered. "It sounds like fun."

A half-hour later, Maisie now in tow, they stood at the foot of the steps, in the Sunset District of the city.

"That woman was right," Hannah said. "I've never seen anything like it." The stairs formed a beautiful, vertical mosaic, starting with scenes from the ocean and leading up to mosaics of the heavens.

Evie nodded. "I'd love to paint it one day," she said.

Hannah said nothing for a moment. "You know, it's inspiring me to do some mosaic pieces, maybe using a mix of sea glass."

"Nice." Evie looked at her friend approvingly, continually awed by her creativity. "Ready to take on the climb?" Evie took the lid off of the latté cup that she had been carrying so that she could better get at the last few drops. She was just about to toss it into the recycling bin when she stopped cold. "Hannah." Her voice was strained.

Hannah was in the midst of doing hamstring stretches. "Hmm?" she said absently, her mind already creating mosaic pendants.

"Hannah!" This time Evie's tone was sharp and Hannah straightened up immediately. "Look." Evie held out the lid, turned over in her palm.

Hannah took a look. And then another.

"What the ...?" She read the message written inside the lid.

From sea to stars, the tiles lead not to Mars
But to Neptune it seems ... as in your dreams.

"I guess," Evie said slowly, "that it's another clue."

"'From sea to stars' ... that's what the stairs depict," Hannah exclaimed. "But what do the stars and planets have to do with all this?"

Evie thought a minute and then snapped her fingers. "Neptune isn't just a planet. Neptune was the Roman god of the sea. And if these stars lead us to Neptune ...

maybe that means that they'll lead us to more mermaid clues."

"Oh, you're good," Hannah said admiringly.

"Know what else I'm good at?" Evie slipped the cup lid into her sweatshirt pocket. "Racing you to the top!"

chapter 31

Ms. Red Hot Nails had been right – the climb was more than worth it.

"You know, this kind of stuff was a lot easier 30 years ago," Hannah complained as she and Evie finally reached the top of the mosaic stairs. From there they climbed a set of cement steps, and then, finally, a small wooden staircase. They topped out at Grandview Park.

"They certainly named this park accurately," Evie answered, a bit winded. "Just look at that view."

Stretched out before them was a view of some of San Francisco's best-loved treasures – the Golden Gate Bridge and Golden Gate Park, of course, as well as the downtown skyline and, in the distance, on the far side of the bridge, the Marin Headlands.

"Did you know that, before the Sunset District was developed and built up in the mid-1900s, it used to be just windswept sand dunes?" Hannah remarked. "And that it gets its name because it's one of the best places to watch the sun set?"

"I didn't," Evie replied. "And look who's doing her homework now."

The two strolled the one-acre park, stopping occasionally to marvel at the view, until finally settling on a bench.

"What a hidden jewel this place is," Evie said.

Hannah nodded.

"Speaking of jewels, how is the Ocean's Enchantment Collection coming along?" Evie asked.

Hannah smiled. "It seems like once we happened upon this mermaid mahjong mystery, my creative spark has really been stoked," she answered. "The sea is like a treasure chest of art and ideas. I can't believe I never thought of it before!"

"I know what you mean," Evie answered. "The Mermaid Mahjong Circle painting was my first foray into working with watercolors." She smiled. "I guess that's apropos, mermaids and water. And now I'm increasingly fascinated with how water affects color – the flow of color, its depth, the layering of shade upon shade."

"It's like you're experiencing a kind of renaissance of your own, Evie," she said reflectively. "It sounds like you're pushing your creative limits outward."

"It does, doesn't it?" Evie was quiet for a moment, trying to take it all in. "There's something else I'm yearning to try art-wise, too," she went on, "although I can't quite see it yet in my mind's eye. I know that it's ocean related, and I know that it feels like this powerful pull in my heart."

"The word 'renaissance' means rebirth," Hannah reasoned to herself. "Is it possible after all these years that we're being reborn as the artists we were always meant to be? And the ocean and mermaids are the key?" she asked, less to Evie and more to the universe.

The two women sat in silence for a few minutes, just trying to absorb their twin epiphanies. Maisie, who had been busy chasing a Painted Lady butterfly that seemed to enjoy teasing her, finally gave up the game and settled with a contented "woof" at Evie's feet. Absently, Evie reached down to scratch behind Maisie's ears – one of the dog's favorite places – when she felt something attached to Maisie's collar.

"What this?" she asked, leaning over to look. A red ribbon was tied to Maisie's collar with a small card attached. The dog rested her head on Evie's knee as she untied the ribbon. The card was painted with the design of a mahjong tile on the front, the message inside scripted in beautiful calligraphy.

"What does it say?" Hannah asked eagerly.

Evie read aloud.

Swim with your heart to find your art
Your Mission is clear – you'll find it here.

"Where did it come from?" Hannah looked around quickly. The only other person nearby was an elderly lady sitting on a bench several yards away and caught up in her knitting. Sensing Hannah's gaze, she looked up quickly, then gathered her things and slipped out of sight in an instant. She looked familiar but it was only several moments later that Hannah realized where she'd seen her before. The dark blue-green eyes gave it away – it was Hai Ling.

chapter 32

"Are you sure?" Evie asked when Hannah recounted what had happened.

"Absolutely," Hannah answered. "We shouldn't be surprised – it's like she and Lorelei are our fairy godmothers. Or should I say fairy godmermaids?"

Evie chuckled. "Good one."

They looked at the clue again.

"Where do we go with this?" Hannah asked.

"It's almost like it's a response to what we've discovered by climbing up here from the 'sea to the stars,'" she replied. "The climb made us aware of how the ocean and its beauty are empowering us and our art. Our reward for making that discovery is this clue."

"Wow." Hannah paused for a moment. "Seems like someone has gone to really great lengths to guide us forward." She grinned. "Or should I say great depths?"

Evie laughed. "Back to the matter at hand." She looked at the message again. "'Swim with your heart to find your art' – surely that must be a reference to mermaids, no?"

"Is it possible that 'your Mission' refers to Mission Dolores?" Hannah asked. "Maybe we need to go there to find out more."

"I haven't been there in years," Evie mused.

She got up and stretched. Maisie did the same.

"Isn't it funny how dogs do their own kind of yoga?" Hannah asked. "She's doing the ultimate, original version of Downward Dog!"

"Leave it to you to come up with that one." Evie chuckled. "She's a lot more flexible than I am these days. I think that the climb up here wore me down a little. She leaned over to scratch Maisie behind her ears, "But Maisie doesn't seem any worse for the wear." Maisie's tail began to wag.

"That's because we're not puppies anymore," Hannah said fondly. "But we still look good."

"Yes, we do," Evie agreed. "Yes, we do." She picked up Maisie's leash and looked out once again at the view. "It certainly is a beautiful city," she said. "I never get tired of seeing it from every angle."

"Spoken like a true artist." Hannah got to her feet slowly. "Race you back down?"

chapter 33

Santa Barbara, Summer of 1971

William and Ella St. John sat on the veranda of their home overlooking the Pacific Ocean. The mild breeze and brilliant sunshine made for a picture-postcard afternoon, the palm trees swaying gently and the ocean waves lapping at the shore. It was the perfect day for a 60th anniversary.

The couple sat in companionable silence, still holding hands after all the years. Ella, her blonde hair turned pure white, was dressed in a lilac-blue dressing gown with silver sandals, sapphires in her ears. Even at 80, she remained a remarkable beauty. William, still a handsome man at 85, wore a linen shirt and slacks, his once-dark hair now silvery.

"I love this place," Ella said happily, savoring the coastline, the roses growing in her abundant garden, and the day itself. "Thank you for bringing us here."

William squeezed her hand gently. "The move was a good idea," he said, nodding his head. "The weather down here is much better for your health."

Ella nodded. The warmer, drier weather was a relief as she had gotten older. The cold, damp winters in San Francisco had taken a toll on her health, resulting in too many episodes of bronchitis and even a bout with pneumonia. The Mediterranean climate of Santa Barbara was like a balm. After moving there just over a year before, she was starting to feel more like herself.

"Is it really 60 years since we've been married?" she asked. "Where has the time gone?"

William shook his head, a small smile on his face. "It's been quite an adventure," he said, looking at her tenderly. "We've raised two amazing daughters, for one," he said. "And remember all the wonderful things we used to do in San Francisco?" he added. "Remember the Panama-Pacific Exposition?"

"Of course!" Ella exclaimed. "I'll never forget the Palace of Fine Arts especially. Remember how, after we saw the Birth of Venus *by Botticelli there, you wanted to name our daughter Venus?" She playfully tapped him on the arm.*

"I do," he said, nodding. "And you know what else I remember?" Here he winked at her. "Our 15th anniversary spent in the penthouse of the Fairmont."

Ella blushed. "Oh, you!" she said, looking up at him from under her eyelashes. "You're still a scoundrel, if only in your thoughts."

He laughed and kissed her on the cheek.

"I'll never forget that romantic night and how gorgeous that penthouse was," she said dreamily. "That's one of my favorite moments of our life together."

"Mine too."

"But my very favorite moment? That would be today," she went on. "And every day that comes after. Every day that I get to spend with you is another gift. We're still here, still together, and still in love. Or at least I am," she joked.

"I've loved you my entire life, Ella," he said softly, a catch in his voice. "I can't remember the years before you became my wife. "You are everything to me."

"Oh, sweetheart," she murmured. "I can't imagine my life without you in it."

He pulled her close and rested his head upon hers. "Neither can I," he said, a catch in his voice.

Then he released her. "I've got an anniversary present for you," he said, reaching into his pocket.

She clapped her hands in joy like a little girl. "What is it?" she asked excitedly.

He pulled out a small red lacquer box and handed it to her.

She admired the beautiful red color and then opened the box. It was lined in gold velvet.

"You know," she said, looking away from the box and at him for a moment. "This box reminds me of something."

He smiled. "It should," he said. "Keep looking inside."

Ella turned her attention back to the box and, a moment later, she gasped in surprise. Nestled in the gold velvet was a charm that resembled a mahjong tile. On it was a delicate etching of a mermaid sitting on a rock, her mirror in hand. Her golden hair billowed around her, and her tail was done in a rainbow of blues and purples. In her hand she clasped a tiny aquamarine.

As Ella lifted the charm from the gold velvet, its platinum chain unfurled. William took the necklace from her and fastened it around her neck.

"But how did you manage to find a charm identical to the mahjong tiles in the set?" Ella asked him, still stunned.

He laughed. "It took some time," he explained. "But I discovered another carver – this one a fascinating woman named Lorelei – who was able to recreate the image I asked for, this time on white jade."

"Darling, it's exquisite," Ella said softly, looking down at the mahjong tile charm dangling from the chain around her neck. "I never expected to see another tile like this again."

"What can I say? I'm a magician!" he said, laughing.

She leaned in to kiss him. "I always thought there was a little bit of magic attached to those tiles," she said. "I don't know why, but they seemed to radiate some kind of energy all their own."

William put his arm around Ella's shoulders and pulled her close to him. "Whatever you do," he whispered into her hair, "don't show it to Pearl. You remember what happened the last time she saw a mermaid mahjong tile!"

Ella laughed in response and snuggled into him. And there they sat, watching as afternoon turned to twilight, together and in love.

chapter 34

The weekend after their adventure in Grandview Park found Evie and Hannah exploring the Mission District, minds open and senses heightened. Walking through the district's streets, they felt as if they, themselves, were part of a tableau. The Mission's street murals embraced them in a blaze of color and movement, transporting them from one to the next on a wave of art. Murals on walls and garage doors – vibrant, moving paintings that spoke to human rights, to global issues, to AIDS awareness and advocacy, and to so much more.

"Is it just me, or do you feel as if we've become part of the picture?" Hannah asked Evie as they stood for a moment before an entire street of mural-fronted buildings.

Hannah nodded, sharing her friend's enthusiasm. "It kind of takes your breath away, doesn't it?" she agreed.

The women continued their walk, bounded on both sides by the pieces of street art that were so much a part of the Mission's heartbeat. They explored Balmy Street, which, they were told by a local shop owner, was where the mural movement began in the Mission. Based on the proprietor's advice, they then walked down Clarion Alley to see more of the area's uniquely original and soulful art offerings.

"How can anyone walk through the Mission and not be inspired, either to create beautiful art or to advocate for a cause?" Hannah wondered aloud.

Evie nodded in agreement. "It doesn't get clearer than right here," she said. "Art for action. Art as an expression of compassion. Art as an instrument of power and change."

Hannah appraised her friend for a moment. "Careful, Evie," she teased. "Your I-wasn't-old-enough-to-be-a-real-hippie-but-I-am-one-in-my-soul side is showing."

Evie gave her a small smile and flashed a V-sign. "Peace, love, and mermaids," she responded as they turned a corner and headed to Mission Dolores.

The Mission stood on 16th Street, where it had been standing since June of 1776, when it was founded by Father Junipero Serra.

"It's the oldest original intact mission of the 21 that were founded in California by Father Serra *and* it's the oldest building in San Francisco," Hannah told Evie. At Evie's surprised look, she explained, "I did some research once we decided to come here. Anyway," she went on, "there are two parts – the original Old Mission and the Basilica portion which came much, much later.

It was rebuilt following the 1906 earthquake and opened in 1918."

"That means that Ella and Pearl St. John might have visited here at some point," Evie said excitedly. "Even if they weren't Catholic, they might have wanted to see the Old Mission as part of the history of their city and the new Basilica as a piece of architectural art."

"That's true." Hannah nodded. "And listen to this – while the Old Mission was a much more modest structure, both in size and décor, it did house a hidden mural that had been created by the Native Americans who had helped to build it."

"A hidden mural?"

"Apparently, it was painted on a main wall of the mission but was covered by an altarpiece – a *reredros* – to protect it from the light and the elements. It was only brought to the public's view for the first time in this century, when the artwork was digitized and then projected on the dome of the Basilica for a few years. Before that, the mural hadn't been seen for more than two centuries."

"A mural," Evie said thoughtfully. "Imagine that."

"Actually, a reproduction of the mural was painted a few years ago on a building just a few blocks from here," Hannah went on. "But sadly, that building was demolished after a fire."

"Wow." Evie seemed lost in thought.

The two friends made their donations and took a short tour through the Old Mission. Then they made their way into the Basilica. Evie stopped in her tracks at her first glance of the magnificent stained-glass windows; Hannah, gazing up at the Basilica dome, walked right into her.

"Ow!" she yelped, bumping into Evie's back.

"What?" Evie asked distractedly, her attention barely swayed from the glorious jewel tones streaming across the church on beams of sunlight. "Hannah – look! Have you ever seen colors like that?"

Hannah followed Evie's pointed finger to the windows ringing the Basilica, each one bedecked with a richness of color that adorned the church with a glorious splendor.

"Those colors," Hannah marveled. "That amazing ruby red," she said looking at one of the windows of four angels, each holding a musical instrument.

"I did some research about stained glass before I visited Europe," Evie said. "Antique red stained glass was actually the rarest and the most expensive to make."

"Because?" Hannah prompted her.

"Because the red color faded more quickly than any other," Evie explained. "In order to get red glass to maintain its color, the red needed to be mixed with gold. That's what made it more costly." She stood in place, twirling to see one window after the next. "These pieces are magnificent, Hannah," she said, awed. "I wish I could create with color like that." She closed her eyes for a moment and, when she opened them, they were sparkling.

"Uh-oh, I feel an idea coming," Hannah said, catching her friend's excitement.

"A stained-glass mural of mermaids," Evie said. "No, wait. A mixed-media mural."

"Nice alliteration," Hannah commented.

"Hmmm?" Evie was still caught up in visions of stained glass. Then she snapped to attention, her mind laser-focused on a new idea. "Maybe there's a piece we can work on together." Her excitement was mounting. "Maybe it's a multi-media piece of art that combines paint and jewels, ink and silk, glass and mosaic ..." Her voice drifted off as she lost herself in her imaginings.

Hannah hugged her. "What an amazing thought!" Her cheeks were pink with excitement and energy. "I'd love to work with you!"

"Something rooted in this mermaid mahjong circle that we seem to be part of," Evie went on. "Something that empowers the women who experience it and motivates them to go out and put power to the kind of beauty that they create." She paused, momentarily out of breath. "Something that tells our story and the story of the women who preceded us here – something that gives other women the chance to tell their story, all through their art."

"A mural," Hannah said softly. "We've got to create a mermaid mural, Evie. And I think I've got the perfect place for it, too," she said.

Evie waited expectantly.

"You know that after my mother died, she left me heir to the entire estate that my father left to her," she explained. At Evie's nod, she went on. "Well, I've been trying to decide where to donate that money, where it could do the most good."

Evie nodded.

"I've just crystallized the idea of what I want to do with it. I want to build a women's arts center. What if we held classes, brought in speakers, hosted exhibits and concerts – you know, music, painting, sculpture, poetry, culinary arts, everything." She stopped and took a breath. "A women's circle for the arts."

"I love the 'circle' idea," Evie said. "Maybe we can incorporate mermaids into the name. After all, we owe all of the inspiration to the mermaid mahjong tiles." She paused a moment. "How about this – The Mermaid Mahjong Circle: A Women's Center for the Arts."

Hannah beamed. "I love it!" she said. Her eyes lit up. "I've done a little bit of reading up on mahjong since all this started, and I think there's a tile that kind of looks like a double M – an M with an upside-down M over it." She scrolled on her tablet. A few seconds later, she showed Evie the screen, barely able to contain her excitement. "Here it is," she said. "It's the Eight Bam tile – it stands for eight sticks of bamboo. And it looks exactly like a double M."

"Wait," Evie said, realization dawning, "Double M for Mermaid Mahjong, right?"

Hannah nodded. "And that," she said happily, "is how a logo is born."

"More than a logo – a way to give women the chance to empower themselves via their artistic expression," Evie said excitedly.

"That's how this all started!" Hannah had a huge smile on her face.

"And if it's a true circle, then it won't have an end."

"Perfect," Hannah said, giving Evie a hug. "Our mural needs to reflect all of it."

Evie nodded. "Maybe we should work on the mural as a bunch of separate canvases or pieces and then join them together as we mount them on the wall of the center. If we do it that way, we can create it in my studio."

"Agreed," Hannah thought for a moment. "I think the mural should be the first thing that visitors see when they enter the arts center – right there in the lobby – big, bold, and beautiful."

"Where do you think you might want to have the arts center built?" Evie asked, curious.

Hannah's eyes lit up as she answered. "There's an old private elementary school in my neighborhood that closed just last year," she explained. "The property has been for sale since then with no takers. It might make the perfect location." She took out her stylus to sketch a diagram of the building on her tablet. "It's big enough for studios and exhibit spaces, and we can use the classrooms for whatever classes we schedule. Plus there's an auditorium for the performances we'd want to offer and a cafeteria that we can convert into a café."

"Or use for cooking classes."

"Or both!"

The two friends stood there, grinning at each other.

"It sounds like you've had this place in mind for a while." Evie commented.

Hannah nodded. "I've been thinking about it ever since I saw the 'For Sale or Lease' sign last year, but I wasn't sure exactly what I could turn it into," she said. "I never imagined something like this – something we could create together that could really make a difference. This could be amazing!" Hannah had tears in her eyes as she thought about their project.

"I think it's a wonderful way to use your inheritance," Evie said softly. "You'll be leaving a truly meaningful legacy."

"You too – we're in this together," Hannah reminded her, wiping her eyes.

Evie nodded, too touched to speak for a moment. Then, "We need to get started," she said. "There are a million details. We're going to need an architect, contractors, lawyers ..." She stopped talking at the look on Hannah's face. "What is it, Hannah?"

Hannah grinned. "I just thought of one more room we're going to need at the arts center." At Evie's questioning look, she finished her thought. "A place to play mahjong."

"Deal." Evie laughed as they made their way out of the Basilica and into the Mission's gift shop. They browsed for a few moments, looking at the postcards depicting scenes from the Mission as well as the devotional candles, rosaries, and crosses.

Just as they were about to leave, a nun, dressed in a traditional habit and wearing dark glasses, came over to Evie and touched her on the arm. "Yes, Sister?" Evie asked her.

The nun smiled. "I just wanted to remind you both that your MUNI bus will be here shortly." Before Evie had a chance to reply, the nun turned and walked away.

Evie grabbed Hannah's arm, her expression one of shock.

"What was that about – why would she think we were going to take a MUNI and how does she know where we might be going?" Hannah asked.

Evie watched as the nun disappeared and then grabbed Hannah's hand and pulled her out onto the street.

"You saw the same nun that I did, right?" she asked Hannah, her voice a bit shaky.

"Of course I did, Evie. What's going on?"

"You noticed that she was dressed in a traditional long black habit, wimple and all."

"Of course I did." Hannah tried to keep the impatience out of her voice but she was anxious to hear what had made Evie so upset.

Evie took a deep breath. "Did you notice that she wasn't wearing the usual kind of rosary around her waist."

"What do you mean?" Hannah asked, urging Evie on.

Evie shook her head. "Right there in the midst of the rosary beads ..."

"What?" Hannah practically shouted. "What?"

"... there was a mahjong tile."

"Seriously?" Hannah could only stare.

Evie nodded slowly. "And you know what else?"

"You mean there's more?"

Evie could barely contain herself. "What kind of shoes do traditional nuns wear with their habits?"

Hannah shrugged. "Plain black ones? I never noticed."

"Exactly!" Evie pointed at Hannah excitedly. "You never noticed because the habits and the shoes aren't meant to draw attention."

"So?" Hannah felt her impatience getting the better of her again. "What's the point?"

"This nun was wearing red pumps."

"No way."

"Way. Obviously, she was no nun." Evie looked amused. "Actually, they were beautiful shoes. Sort of a claret-red snakeskin leather on a narrow stacked heel. I've seen them somewhere before, not that long ago, but I can't say where."

Now it was Hannah's turn to look a bit shocked.

"Han?"

"You saw them on Delia Charlton," Hannah said softly. "I noticed them when she came out of the store to talk to us and showed us her mahjong tile necklace. Looks like she followed us here."

"Another visit from one of the tile wearers," Evie said pensively.

"Evie, look!"

Evie looked up and followed the direction of Hannah's pointing finger. A MUNI bus was just passing by. Where an ad would usually go on its side was a panel reading:

MERMAID MISSION POSSIBLE

"Oh my," Evie said slowly, shaking her head. "Seems like someone is telling us that our mission to build the Mermaid Mahjong Circle arts center is not just a whim."

"This calls for some sugar," Hannah said. "Stat."

chapter 35

delia's tale

My name is Cordelia. Actually, this is my mermaid name. My land name is Delia – it's much easier for ordinary people to remember, especially my customers.

I was the owner of a tiny bridal boutique in San Francisco, specializing in one-of-a-kind, vintage bridal wear. What made these pieces one-of-a-kind is that they were all made by hand by women artisans. What made them vintage? These pieces were crafted a long time ago – sometimes as long as hundreds of years. What made them special is that I procured some of them centuries ago and saved them to sell in my store.

Whether bridal veils or purses, earrings or bracelets, satin dancing shoes or delicately embroidered negligées, all of these were available in my store – and all were collected by me when brides from the 1700s through the 1800s and early 1900s were through with them. Certainly, even brides of that day saved their gowns for daughters or granddaughters, but you'd be surprised at how many of them didn't give a second thought to the accessories that they wore on their big day.

I was a laundress in the home of many a fine lady in those years, and, after a bit of experience, I developed a sense for which brides would be keeping tabs on their wedding-day finery and which would not. Was I a common thief? I prefer to think of myself as a woman of skill with an enhanced ability for quick-handedness and ingenuity. I would take these pieces when the brides were off on their honeymoons; in my vast experience, when they would first think to inquire after their bridal possessions would be several years later, if at all. And by that time, I was gone.

How I came to this occupation is a story indeed. I was born in Spain around 1700 or so to a father who was a wealthy silk merchant and a mother who loved to spend his money. I was beautiful and reckless, so that it was no surprise that I became pregnant at sixteen – or so I thought. Despairing of the black mark that my pregnancy would leave on the family name, my parents were quick to pack me up and send me away to the Caribbean immediately.

I boarded a galleon bound for Jamaica, where my father's distant cousin and his wife lived and agreed to take me in, for a sizable payment from my father, of course. The plan was for me to give birth on the island, where everyone would be told that I was a widow, and then live there on the money that my father would settle upon me. With any luck, my parents hoped, I would marry a rich importer and live respectfully, if not happily, ever after.

But the best laid plans often go awry. As it turned out, I was no more with child than was the ship's captain, a truth that was revealed a few days out at sea. As if that were not a big enough shock, what followed certainly was. Our ship was attacked by pirates not long afterward and, instead of being afraid, I found myself attracted to these thieves of the sea. In a move echoed by Errol Flynn in so many pirate movies, one very handsome buccaneer wrapped his arm around my waist and swung me over from the galleon to the pirate ship on a rope. Very dashing. And very exciting.

I sailed back to Jamaica aboard the pirate ship and, once there, decided to avoid living with my relatives. I found a job as a bar maid instead, and enjoyed the company of many a man of the sea. But I couldn't stay still, entranced as I was by the stories that I heard every night. One night, Anne Bonny, the famous woman pirate, strolled into the tavern with her pirate lover, Calico Joe. After hearing about just a few of her adventures, I knew that I wanted to become a pirate myself. Two days later found me with my hair cropped short, wearing men's clothing, and talking my way aboard her ship as a lowly worker.

And so my pirating life began and, I'm afraid to say, I was very good at it. I stuck solely to robbing passengers of their jewels and furs, silks and satins, and anything else of value. I drew the line at hurting anyone and, somehow, I got away with it.

It seemed that Lady Luck was with me until the day she wasn't. We had just boarded a galleon and set about to create mayhem and take whatever we wanted. I must have let my guard down for a moment, because suddenly I found myself at the wrong end of a swing gun that had been mounted on the ship's side but was now in the hands of one of the ship's crew. And he was seething,

I had no time to think or run. It was either be shot or jump into the sea. I chose the latter but, before I had the chance to do so, I found myself aided by the side of the gun, slammed into my head, killing me even before I had the chance to drown.

And that was it. Until it wasn't.

I came to under the sea where an angel – Lorelei that is – held me in her arms and gently stroked my forehead where it had been bludgeoned, healing me back to life. Around me, as I opened my eyes, I saw a circle of mermaids, each shimmering with color and each holding out her arms to welcome me into their world.

From there I became one of them. And while I went back to land time and again over the centuries to help myself to bridal finery in the guise of a laundress, I always returned to the sea. Finally, I opened my little store in San Francisco, just to draw Evie and Hannah in. If you look for the store now, you'll see that it has disappeared. Much the same way that Lorelei's cottage in Half Moon Bay is no longer there.

Call it a little bit of mermaid magic.

chapter 36

"Mmmm, what are these?" Hannah asked through a mouthful of crumbs. "These are sensational!" The two friends were settled in Evie's kitchen.

Evie smiled. "They're called *Orange You a Mermaid?* meringues," she answered. "They're good, huh?"

"I'd say so," Hannah said after another bite. "Is that really the recipe name?"

Evie nodded. "It's strange, though," she said. "I was going through my recipe file, such as it is, looking for the recipe for those amazing brownies I used to make – you know, the ones with the butterscotch and chocolate chips and the caramel topping?"

Hannah looked as if she were about to swoon at the thought.

"And then, on the back of that recipe, just sticking to it, was this one." She looked a bit puzzled. "I have to admit, though, I don't ever remember making these cookies or even pulling the recipe out of a magazine. Frankly, I have no idea where it came from."

Hannah just stared at her. "You're telling me that a mysterious recipe called *Orange You a Mermaid?* meringues just showed up from nowhere?"

Evie nodded. "I know it sounds strange."

Hannah snorted. "Strange? It sounds like our favorite mermaid expert somehow put it there."

"You mean Lorelei?"

Hannah nodded her head, her silvery curls bobbing.

Evie sat down on a kitchen stool. "Lorelei really, really, really wants us to believe in this mermaid fantasy. I guess I'm just impatient to see the outcome."

"I could tell you that good things come to those who wait." Evie made a face at the old adage. "Or," Hannah continued, "I could say that, in the meantime, why don't we have another cookie?"

Evie giggled. "You crack me up," she told her friend, passing the platter. "Here you go."

"How do you make them?" Hannah asked. "Not that I ever bake, but I'm just curious about the flavors."

"They're basic meringue cookies – egg whites, sugar, vanilla extract. But in this recipe, you also add some semi-sweet chocolate chips and some orange extract. It's the chocolate and the orange that make them so, so yummy."

Hannah nodded as she reached for her third cookie.

"And they're really light so that you can eat a few and not do too much damage," Evie said, joining her friend in reaching for another.

"And the name is so darn cute," Hannah said. "Hey, Evie?"

"Yes?"

"Thanks for making them. And, orange you a mermaid?"

Hannah ducked as Evie's napkin sailed above her head.

Hannah reached for another napkin from a basket on the table. As she did, a slip of paper slid to the floor. She bent forward and scooped it up. Then she turned it over in her hands and just stared.

"Hannah?" Evie asked. "What is it?"

"Here. Read it." Hannah held it out.

Evie grabbed her reading glasses off the top of her head and examined the slip.

A strand of pearls is not complete
Until the Center one you meet.

"Who said anything about pearls?" Evie asked.

Hannah shook her head, puzzled. "Don't know," she said. "And why is 'Center' uppercase? Is it a place?"

Evie was silent for a moment and then snapped her fingers. "Maybe it is!" she exclaimed. "Maybe it stands for our new women's center for the arts."

Hannah just stared at her. "Now what?" she asked weakly.

Evie shook her head. "The plot thickens."

chapter 37

The morning fog was just about to roll back over the Golden Gate Bridge a few days later as Evie and Hannah made their way to Marin, Maisie happily perched on the back seat of the Jeep, her nose pressed against the partially open back window. A bakery box from Schubert's rested on the floor at Hannah's feet. Its precious cargo was an opera cake, redolent with the aromas of chocolate, hazelnut, and praline.

"Thanks for coming with me today to visit Great-Aunt Vennie," Evie said, eyes on the road. "I try to see her every couple of months. But this is the first time I've visited her in her new home outside the city. It's nice to have company."

"You didn't have to ask me twice," Hannah said happily. "Not once you mentioned that we were going to stop at Schubert's on the way."

"Aunt Vennie loves their opera cake. She's been eating it since she was a little girl." Evie slowed slightly as the road led through the Robin Williams Tunnel into brilliantly sunny Marin.

"How old is she again?" Hannah asked.

"Somewhere between 100 and heaven." Evie smiled. "That's how she answers that question, although I wouldn't advise you asking it. She's not really my great-aunt – she was a lifelong friend of my grandmother's. I remember her and her husband visiting with my grandmother and grandfather whenever I got to sleep over at their house. Aunt Vennie always brought an opera cake from Schubert's. And she always let me try on her pearl necklaces and bracelets."

Hannah laughed. "I don't see you as the pearl type," she said. "Emeralds, certainly; but pearls? Nope."

Evie grinned back, her green eyes crinkling at the edges with good humor. "Good call," she said. "Pearls aren't my thing these days. But back then, when I was a little girl playing dress up? They were perfect. There's a photo of me somewhere where I managed to wind myself from head to toe in her ropes of pearls. I'm wearing a pair of her high heels and I've got her red lipstick all over my face because I put it on myself." She chuckled. "Maybe that's why that message mentioned pearls. Although I don't get the connection."

"I think my brain needs a break from the mermaid deluge, pardon the pun," Hannah said.

"I'm with you." Evie put on her signal. "Look. Here's our exit."

They drove for another mile until they reached the discreet sign and towering oaks that marked the entrance to Aunt Vennie's senior-living complex.

"Wow, this is lovely," Hannah commented as they wound past small, Italianate-style villas, each surrounded by flowering shrubs, manicured lawns, and stone walkways.

Evie nodded. "It is. Luckily, Aunt Vennie came from a well-to-do family, as did Uncle Lester, so money isn't a problem for her now. After he died ten years ago, she continued to live in their home in Sea Cliff but then decided to move out here just a few months ago – along with her younger sister, Elizabeth." Here she giggled. "Although it's not like Elizabeth isn't at least 95 herself. The two of them together are quite the sketch."

Hannah chortled. "That'll be us one day. Two old ladies talking about the good old days and winking at the pool boys."

"You're such a pig!" Evie shook her head as she turned into the private driveway in front of Aunt Vennie's place.

"You say that now, but that's what will keep us young," Hannah said, gathering her purse and grabbing the cake box. "Just wait."

Aunt Vennie opened the door a split second after Evie knocked. A tiny woman dressed in a signature Chanel rose-colored tweed suit – pearls galore – she barely reached Evie's chin, even in her high heels. Her silver hair was held off her face by a deep red velvet headband and her turquoise-colored eyes sparkled with good humor.

"Darling, it's so good to see you!" She gave Evie a huge hug and then opened her arms to Hannah. "And you must be Hannah – I've heard lots of good things about you. And some naughty things too!" She wagged her perfectly manicured fingertip at Hannah and gave her a huge smile.

Hannah hugged this sprite of a woman back, totally taken by Aunt Vennie's undeniable charm. "I could say the same right back to you, Mrs. Harper."

"Mrs. Harper?" Aunt Vennie shook her chicly coiffed head. "Whenever I hear that name, I look for my mother-in-law, bless her soul. Please call me Aunt Vennie – I insist. And this is my younger sister, Elizabeth."

Elizabeth Ames stood just a couple of steps behind Aunt Vennie. The family resemblance was there, although it was clear that Vennie was the firebrand of the two. Dressed in a similar suit – albeit in a cream and gray tweed – Elizabeth smiled shyly and shook Hannah's hand. She gave a little wave to Evie.

Maisie nuzzled Elizabeth's hand and was rewarded with a pat on her head. The dog immediately decided that Elizabeth was her new best friend.

"Come along," Aunt Vennie said, looping one arm through Evie's and holding a cane in her other hand as she led the way to the small dining room. "Let's enjoy our lunch and then I'll show you around the rest of the villa."

The women dined on homemade quiche and basil corn muffins along with a crisp salad dressed with lemon vinaigrette. For dessert, Aunt Vennie poured cups of Lady Grey tea to sip with the opera cake which she pronounced, "Exquisite!"

"This was all delicious," Evie said afterward. "Who is the chef?"

Aunt Vennie's laugh was like a little chirp. "Neither of us," she admitted. "My housekeeper, Birgitta, also serves as our cook. Lucky for us or else we'd starve, right, Elizabeth?"

Aunt Vennie giggled and Elizabeth's lips curved up into a small smile. "Right, indeed," she agreed.

"Now, who'd like the Grand Tour?" Aunt Vennie slowly pulled herself up from her chair with the help of her cane. Evie got up to help her and, as she glanced down at the cane's handle, her eyes widened.

The handle was the head of mermaid, crafted of sterling silver. Her long hair swirled around her face, neck, and upper body. Her tail, carved of mahogany, featured overlapping scales and extended down the length of the entire cane. The mermaid's eyes were blue-green gems – aquamarine if Evie had to guess – and her tail glinted with a sprinkling of tiny crystals set into the wood.

"Dear, are you all right?" Aunt Vennie stood in front of a motionless Evie. "Evie? Is something wrong?"

"What? Oh, no, no," Evie said, recovering her voice. "I was just admiring your cane."

"My walking stick, you mean," Aunt Vennie said, pulling herself up to her full height of less than five feet. "Canes are for old people!"

"Of course," Evie said giving Vennie her arm to hold. "Hannah," she said, shooting her friend a look. "Take a look at this beautiful walking stick."

Hannah, who had been slowly drawing Elizabeth out of her shyness by asking questions about her past, excused herself for a moment and stepped over to Evie and Aunt Vennie. One look at the walking stick, and the expression on her face told Evie that she was not alone in her amazement. "That's a remarkable piece of carving, Aunt Vennie," Hannah said. "Wherever did you find it?"

But Aunt Vennie had moved on from the conversation and seemed eager to show Evie and Hannah her home. They toured the country-style kitchen; Elizabeth's elegant bedroom and sitting area done up in tones of taupe and silver; and a luxuriously comfortable living room filled with overstuffed couches and chairs in velvet, complemented by several brilliantly colored handwoven rugs. Finally, they reached Aunt Vennie's suite. When they entered, Evie and Hannah shared another look.

The walls of the room were covered in silk the color of seafoam. A king-sized bed, mounded with pillows in ivory, seafoam, palest coral, and deep amethyst, stood against one wall, while a loveseat covered in ivory brocade ran alongside another. A vanity table done in ivory and gold with a rose-cushioned seat was near one of the windows; it held a group of colorful, intricately cut crystal perfume bottles that turned the rays of the afternoon sun into a million rainbows on the wall, and a jeweled hairbrush.

A white marble mantle shot through with veins of silver and gold graced a small fireplace across from the bed. On the wall above it hung a small oil painting.

Evie stepped closer, recognition dawning on her face. It was a perfect reproduction of one of the most famous paintings of all time – Botticelli's *The Birth of Venus.*

"This room is just beautiful, Aunt Vennie," Evie said, twirling slowly to see it all.

"It reminds me of something but I can't quite put my finger on it," Hannah said thoughtfully. "Something about the colors …"

"I imagine it reminds you a bit of the colors in Lorelei's sitting room," Vennie said with a sniff. "She's always stealing my ideas about décor."

Evie lunged to catch Hannah's mug of tea before she dropped it on the white rug out of shock.

"You know Lorelei?" Evie asked haltingly.

"Silly girl, of course I do." Aunt Vennie looked surprised at the question. "I thought she had told you all about me."

Evie and Hannah shook their heads as one.

Then, "When did you meet?" Hannah asked, holding her tea with both hands to avoid any further incident.

Aunt Vennie went over to the loveseat and plunked herself down with a small "oof."

"You know some days, I really feel my age," she said. She gestured to Elizabeth who was perched on the dressing-table seat. "Are you feeling okay, Lizzie?" she asked solicitously.

"Just a little bit tired," Elizabeth answered with a yawn. She smiled at Evie and Hannah. "It's been wonderful meeting you girls, but I do believe my afternoon nap is calling me." She got up to leave the room. "Don't wear them out, Vennie," she teased. "They've got to drive back to the city later on."

"Oh, go on with you," Aunt Vennie replied with a shooing motion. "That woman just cannot stop telling me what to and not to do." But her smile conveyed the affection that she had for her sister. "She just can't help herself," she said fondly as Elizabeth left the room, "although I'm older and she should have to listen to me!"

Evie and Hannah settled themselves on Aunt Vennie's' bed, moving aside some of the cushions to make room.

"So, Aunt Vennie, how is it that you and Lorelei know each other?" Evie asked again in what she hoped was a casual tone.

"Oh, we met ages ago," Aunt Vennie said, kicking off her pumps and tucking her feet under herself. "She looked about my mother's age then and I was a little, little girl."

"But Aunt Vennie," Evie said gently. "Lorelei looks – well, I don't know how old she looks – but it's hard to believe that she is that much older than you."

"Not that you don't look amazing for your age," Hannah chimed in. "Or for any age," she quickly added, seeing Vennie's fleeting look of irritation.

"Lorelei is most definitely older than me," Aunt Vennie insisted. "Centuries."

Hannah rolled her eyes at the hyperbole.

"Okay, okay," Evie said, trying to soothe Aunt Vennie's ruffled feathers.

Aunt Vennie sniffed indignantly. "Mermaid magic," she said under her breath.

"Aunt Vennie?" Evie looked the older woman straight in the eye. "What did you say?"

Aunt Vennie looked from Evie to Hannah. Then she smiled.

"You're right, girls," she said then. "Lorelei does look younger than me. That's because she's a mermaid."

Hannah dropped her now-empty mug. "She's what?" she nearly shouted.

Evie hurried to pick up the mug and placed it on the nightstand. "What do you mean?"

"I mean, she's a mermaid." Aunt Vennie shook her head stubbornly. "And no, I'm not getting absent-minded or suffering from old age." She stood up and stamped her little foot. "Lorelei is a mermaid. And so is Hai Ling. And so is Cordelia Charlton – or Delia, as she goes by when she's on land."

"I don't believe this," Hannah whispered.

"But – but –" Evie couldn't find the words.

"But how did you meet?" Hannah stepped in. "I mean, I can't believe I'm asking this, but how does a little girl meet a mermaid if not through a bedtime story?"

Aunt Vennie frowned at Hannah but couldn't hold the expression for long. "I know it sounds fantastical," she began. "But given that you've already met Lorelei,

Hai Ling, and Delia, you're probably used to hearing things that aren't – well – exactly logical or scientific."

Evie and Hannah sat transfixed, hanging onto her every word.

"I guess you could say that I'm the one responsible for all those mahjong tiles floating around," she said thoughtfully. "It's just that I've always loved mermaids, and once I saw that set – with each tile depicting a beautiful mermaid in a different pose – I couldn't help myself. I just couldn't not play with them."

Evie listened to Aunt Vennie's words, her mind working overtime. There was something bothering her about the account, something tickling her memory – something she just couldn't name.

"So, on that morning, I realized it was my last chance to set the mermaids free," Aunt Vennie was saying matter-of-factly.

"Aunt Vennie!" Evie broke in sharply. "I've never asked you before, but 'Vennie' is such an unusual name. "Is it short for something? Venessa? Venetia? Deven? Lavenia?"

Hannah turned to Evie. "Shh, she's in the middle of the story," she said, perched on the edge of the bed.

"Sorry to interrupt, Aunt Vennie," Evie went on. "But I really need to know."

Aunt Vennie looked at Evie appraisingly. "You're so sharp, Evie." She smiled a little guiltily. "'Vennie' is short for 'Venus,' and it's the name I've gone by for years."

"But that's not your first name," Evie said, her voice beginning to tremble.

"No, I'm afraid not, my dear," Aunt Vennie said quietly. "My first name is Pearl. When Lorelei met me, my full name was Pearl Venus St. John."

Evie gasped.

Hannah shrieked and fell off the bed.

Maisie covered her eyes with her paws.

chapter 38

"So, Lorelei and Hai Ling and Delia are all mermaids," Evie said slowly, trying to let the fact absorb.

Aunt Vennie nodded her head encouragingly.

"And all of them have one of the mahjong tiles," Evie went on.

"As do I," Aunt Vennie added. "I kept one," she said impishly.

"I understand the connection between those three women and you," Evie said, "but why do Hannah and I have tiles too?"

"Lorelei, Hai Ling, and Delia are all artists in their own right," Vennie explained. "Hai Ling is an artist of cuisine, Delia is an artist with the loom, and Lorelei ..." here she paused. "Lorelei practices the art of love like no one else."

Evie and Hannah just looked at Aunt Vennie, too surprised to say a word.

"Now I," Aunt Vennie went on as if she hadn't dropped such a surprise in Evie and Hannah's laps,

"I developed my fascination with mermaids from my mother, Ella. And she developed hers –"

"From her mother, who got it from Angélique, who was my great-grandmother," Evie finished.

"That's right, dear," Aunt Vennie said.

"But how does that apply to Hannah and me?" Evie asked again.

"I was just getting to that, Evie," Aunt Vennie said, settling in more comfortably on her loveseat. "The mermaids are very devoted to the arts, although that's not something they're necessarily known for."

"True," Hannah said. "When I think of mermaids, I think of underwater beauties swimming around, riding on seahorses, and brushing their long luxurious hair."

"Exactly!" Aunt Vennie said. "But these mermaids – the mermaids in the Mermaid Mahjong Circle – are special. To them, art is their heart. You can see it in the poses of Hai Ling's grandmother on the mahjong tiles." Then, at the two other women's puzzled looks, she added, "Yes, Hai Ling's grandmother wasn't just a model for the mermaid tiles. She is a mermaid herself." She smiled. "Her name is Meili."

"Did you actually meet Meili?"

Aunt Vennie smiled. "I did. I was lucky enough to meet all of them in their mermaid form a long time ago."

Evie and Hannah stared at her.

"What does that even mean?" Hannah asked.

Aunt Vennie sighed. "I know it sounds strange, to say the least, but Lorelei and Meili were born mermaids, just like Angélique," she said.

"My great-grandmother was a true mermaid?" Evie asked, shocked.

Aunt Vennie nodded. "But not Hai Ling. She became a mermaid under Meili's guidance. The same way that Cordelia became one thanks to Lorelei. And I had the chance when Lorelei first brought me down to the mermaids' kingdom, but I decided I'd rather stay on land."

"Mermaids' kingdom? Is she kidding?" Hannah said to Evie.

"No, I am *not* kidding," Aunt Vennie said, an imperious tone in her voice. "I'll have you know that I was this close to becoming a mermaid and living forever." She held her perfectly manicured thumb and pointer finger barely a quarter-inch apart.

"What changed your mind?" Evie asked softly.

Aunt Vennie gave a small, wistful smile. "When Lorelei asked me the first time, I had just met Lester and was caught up in the romance. I couldn't imagine leaving him, even for a short time. The next time she asked, I was just about to marry Lester. I was in the midst of planning my wedding, and there was nothing more important to me. The third time came soon after we had bought the house in Sea Cliff. I was all caught up in furnishing it and in becoming the perfect society hostess." She smiled at the memory.

"Did she ever ask you again?" This from Hannah.

Aunt Vennie's eyes misted, and it was as if a cloud came over her. "The last time she asked was just a few years ago. Lester had taken ill with Alzheimer's, and I couldn't bear the thought of being out of his presence. I knew that the moment would soon come when he might not recognize me, and I didn't want to waste even a precious second." She pulled a fine linen handkerchief embroidered with a delicate seashell design from her sleeve and dabbed at her tears.

"And now?" Hannah asked gently.

"Now it is too late," Aunt Vennie said. "Lorelei still offers, but I have no desire to become young again the way mermaids can. And I do not want to be immortal – my goodness, I've already outlived all my friends. I only want to be with Lester; if no longer in this life, then certainly in the afterlife." She sniffled and then gave them a big smile. "I leave the mermaiding to younger women like you two."

Evie reached out and took Aunt Vennie's hand.

"But, out of respect for Lorelei and her mermaid circle, I always wear something red, just in case."

"In case of what?" Evie asked.

"In case I have a lapse in judgment one day and choose to return to the mermaids and become one of them," she explained. "Wearing red ensures that I can return to the sea and the mermaid kingdom again after that very first visit all those years ago."

"Wearing red does that?" Hannah tried to jump up from the bed, caught her foot in the bedspread, and went sprawling.

"Doesn't everyone know that?" Aunt Vennie asked, surprised. "In the old days, legend tells us that it used to be a red cape or a red cap, but now any kind of piece of clothing or accessory will do. Once you return from your visit, you must wear or carry something red every day going forward. Otherwise, you'll lose your ability to return for good."

Evie helped Hannah disentangle herself from the blanket and returned to her spot on the bed. Hannah remained sitting on the floor next to Maisie.

"That explains it then," Hannah continued as if nothing had happened.

"What's that?" Evie asked.

"That explains all the red we've been seeing," Hannah said. "When we first met Lorelei, she was wearing that gauzy red dress – you know that floaty thing."

"I remember."

"And Hai Ling had on that crimson-colored satin Chinese dress."

"The cheongsam."

"Right. And Delia was wearing those gorgeous deep red-colored pumps," Hannah said excitedly.

"And you're wearing a red velvet headband, Aunt Vennie!"

Aunt Vennie smiled.

"But Elizabeth isn't wearing red," Hannah said suddenly. "Does she know about the Mermaid Mahjong Circle?

Aunt Vennie shook her head. "Elizabeth was such a shy and anxious child that my mother felt it was better not to fill her head with mermaid imaginings," she explained. "I do adore her, but I make sure not to involve her in any of this." She smiled patiently. "The idea of the Mermaid Mahjong Circle would probably make her head spin."

"It's making my head spin," Hannah admitted.

"Me too," Evie agreed. "But we're so close – I know it."

Aunt Vennie smiled slyly at the two younger women.

"You know, I really loved the opera cake you brought," she said, a gleam in her eye. "But you know what other dessert I can't resist?"

Evie shook her head, waiting for Aunt Vennie to answer her own question.

"Those delightful cookies – you know, the *Orange You a Mermaid?* meringue ones."

"You know about those?" Hannah practically squeaked.

Aunt Vennie laughed. "I do. And I love them," she said. "Any chance you've made them recently, Evie?"

Evie eyed the older woman carefully. "Apparently, you know that I have," she said, waiting for something, although she wasn't sure exactly what.

Aunt Vennie laughed delightedly and clapped her hands together. "Well, then you must realize that you've met the center pearl in the story strand you've been following."

"A strand of pearls is not complete until the Center one you meet," Evie said softly. "That's what was written on the slip of paper we discovered while eating those cookies!"

"Imagine that," Aunt Vennie said. "I'm the center Pearl."

"Of course!" Hannah clapped her hands and leapt to her feet, barely missing tripping over the shoes that she had kicked off earlier.

"Now that you've figured out that part of the story, it won't be long until the rest is revealed," Aunt Vennie continued cryptically. "If I know mermaid logic, it won't be long at all."

"Mermaid logic? You mean that's a thing?" Hannah asked, incredulous.

"Don't be silly, darling," Aunt Vennie said, patting Hannah's hand. "Of course, it's a thing. Mermaids have their own way of thinking, their own sense of timing, their own way of storytelling. And the mermaids in this circle are a unique group."

Evie and Hannah just stared at her.

"It was so good of you to come all the way out here to visit," Aunt Vennie went on. She reached for her cane. "But it's time for you to make your way back home." She tapped the cane on the floor three times, waking Maisie. The dog looked up expectantly, tail wagging.

"But we don't need to leave just yet," Evie said.

"Oh, but you do." Aunt Vennie stood up and began walking from the room. Seeing no other choice, Evie and Hannah followed, Maisie bringing up the rear.

In the driveway, Aunt Vennie stopped and gave each of the younger women a warm hug. "Here, don't forget this," she said, pressing an envelope into Evie's hand. "You'll need this to get to where you're going."

"Aunt Vennie?" Evie asked questioningly.

"No questions," Aunt Vennie said, shooing them out. "Just remember to keep your hearts open." She paused for a moment, tears coming to her eyes. "I know you'll both make the right decision when the time comes." She turned and walked away, leaving Evie and Hannah with more questions to be answered.

chapter 39

Travel the miles to the last of the tiles
The treasure you'll reach on a moonlit beach.

"Well that's not terribly helpful," Hannah commented after reading aloud the message in the envelope that Aunt Vennie had given to Evie. "Which beach? And which night?"

Evie just shook her head as she continued to drive back to the city. "Where's Lorelei when you need her?" she asked.

At that moment Hannah's phone buzzed with an incoming text. She grabbed it, read the text, and then took in a deep breath.

"What is it, Han?" Evie asked tiredly.

"The text says, '*Tomorrow night. Midnight. Bring the packages that Delia gave you. Don't be late. P.S. I know you'll find the right beach.*'"

"I'm guessing that was Lorelei, there when we needed her," Evie said dryly.

"But which beach?"

"The only one that makes sense, given all we've been through, is Half Moon Bay," Evie said thoughtfully.

Hannah's phone buzzed again.

No, the text read.

"Are you kidding me?" Hannah shrieked.

"What now?" Evie asked,

"The text says '*no*' to Half Moon Bay. How is Lorelei doing this?"

"Seriously?" Evie pulled in to a vacant parking spot on the street to continue the conversation.

"How does she know what we're saying? And how does she have my phone number?"

At that last comment, Evie burst out in laughter. "Having your phone number seems to be the least of our questions, given all this," she said, struggling to get the words out between giggles. "I mean, we're talking mermaid logic here!"

At that, Hannah joined in the somewhat hysterical laughing. Maisie, sensing something not quite right with her mommy and her aunt Hannah, began to whimper.

"Oh, no, we're scaring the dog," Evie said, suddenly serious. She reached around to the back seat to pat Maisie's head. "It's okay, Mais," she said softly. "Everything's okay."

The dog gave Evie's hand a couple of licks, then settled back down.

Evie looked at her friend. "I don't have an answer that makes sense, Hannah," she told her friend. "I guess that, as far as this adventure goes, we're in for a penny, in for a pound."

"You mean if we're buying the whole mermaid thing, we need to go along with some of the stranger things that are happening – like the texts."

Evie nodded, continuing to stroke Maisie's thick fur.

"Okay, so if it's not the beach at Half Moon Bay, then where?"

Evie said nothing, lost in thought.

"Boy, what I wouldn't give right now for one of those *Orange You a Mermaid?* cookies that you baked," Hannah said. "I'm starved."

Evie sat up with a start. "What did you just say?" she asked.

"I said that I'm starved."

"No, before that."

"I said I'd love one of those cookies – "

"That I baked," Evie finished for her. "Baked. *Baker* Beach!"

"Huh?"

"Think about it, Hannah. Lorelei put that recipe in with my others. Aunt Vennie knew that I had baked those cookies. Baked. Baked. *Baker* Beach."

Hannah was silent. The phone buzzed again.

Clever girl, the text read.

chapter 40

For as far as the eye could see, the beach was empty, except for Hannah and Evie. A brilliant full moon cast beams that glinted off the waves like shards of platinum. Occasionally, the moonlight caught on the silver-blonde strands of Hannah's hair or turned Evie's eyes from hazel to blue-green. The moonbeams wrapped them both in a pearly glow.

Evie pulled her Cal sweatshirt around her a bit more tightly as an ocean breeze blew across the beach, bringing with it the hazy outline of another woman. As if emerging from a veil of fog, she suddenly became clear.

"Look!" Evie said. "There's Lorelei!"

"Hello again," Lorelei said as she sat down next to Evie. "Are you ready?"

Evie felt herself shiver involuntarily. "Ready?"

"Tonight all will be revealed." Lorelei smiled at her. "There's no need to be nervous," she said gently. "I promised you both that if you opened your minds and hearts to the universe and to all the signs it sent you, then you would be rewarded with a creative inspiration and revelation unlike any other."

"But why are we sitting on a beach at midnight?" Hannah asked. "Couldn't you just have revealed everything over dinner? Maybe in a nice, warm, indoor café?"

Lorelei laughed, a peal somewhere between a crystal bell and a dolphin's greeting. "Oh, Hannah," she said fondly, "you do remind me so much of her."

"Of whom?" Hannah asked, curious.

Lorelei didn't answer. Instead she asked, "Did you bring the packages with you?"

When Hannah and Evie nodded, she directed them to open the small, newspaper-wrapped boxes that Delia had given them weeks earlier. They each tore through the paper to find a small red lacquer box inside. At a nod from Lorelei, they lifted the lids.

Evie and Hannah looked at each other quizzically and then turned to Lorelei. Each box held a little red pouch on a silken cord with a tiny pair of beautifully carved dice, set with rubies, inside.

"What –?" Hannah began but Lorelei shook her head.

"You'll need these for where we're going," she said. "Wear them around your neck."

"We're going to Vegas?" Hannah couldn't keep herself from giggling.

Evie silenced her with a look.

"Just injecting a little humor," Hannah said meekly.

"And you just might find them vital when we return," Lorelei finished.

Evie and Hannah nodded, wide-eyed.

"Well, then," Lorelei stood and removed the scarlet-colored shawl that she had been wearing. Holding one end in each hand, she lifted her arms up and spread them wide, all the while spinning in a circle.

"Sisters of the sea, sisters of the sea, return to me, return to me," she intoned.

Evie and Hannah sat silently, taking it all in and watching as Lorelei spun faster, becoming a blur of color. All at once the sand whirled up and around them, carrying bits of shell and seaweed, starfish and sea glass, in its spin. Then, just as suddenly as the whirlwind began, it calmed. Surrounding the women was a circle of beautiful mermaids, each utterly enchanting and each with a red ribbon in her hair.

"They – I – how?" Hannah stammered as Evie pinched herself to make sure she was awake.

"Hannah, Evie, are you all right?" Lorelei asked, her eyes sparkling. Mutely, they nodded.

"Are these …" Hannah tried again.

"Mermaids? Yes," Lorelei responded.

Evie found herself staring at one of the mermaids who was looking for something inside a tiny purse tied to her waist. Finding it, she held it out for Evie to see. It was a mahjong tile with a mermaid etched on one side, holding a tiny aquamarine. She looked at Evie questioningly.

Evie pulled her mahjong tile necklace out from under her sweatshirt so that the mermaid could see it. Their eyes met. They smiled. And suddenly Evie felt her reality – and the ground under her feet – shift.

It felt like just seconds later that a breeze began, shifting the sands on the beach into a pattern of circles, causing the mermaids to float on air, held aloft as if they were gliding through the sea. Suddenly, from out of nowhere, a myriad of rainbow bubbles appeared, surrounding the mermaids, Lorelei, and Evie and Hannah with a joyful play of light and color.

Evie and Hannah stood there, dumbfounded, as one of the tiny bubbles began to grow. And grow. And grow. The next thing that they knew, they were inside the bubble, peering out at the beach and the seascape. Lorelei was inside the bubble, too, motioning to the mermaids.

At once, the mermaids all lifted the bubble – as if it were weightless – and floated with it to the ocean. They carefully placed it atop the waves as they dove underneath it. Then each mermaid pulled the long red ribbon from her hair and wrapped it around the floating bubble.

"Pinch me," Hannah said softly to Evie. "Am I awake? Is this really happening?"

"I think so," Evie answered. "But I feel like we're living inside one of those beautiful fairy-tale books we owned when we were kids."

Hannah nodded. "Look!" she said. "We're moving!"

Sure enough, once all the red hair ribbons had been wrapped around the bubble, the mermaids grabbed the free ends and then began pulling the bubble down, down, down toward the ocean's floor.

"Oh!" Evie's eyes could not have been bigger in her face. "I can't believe this!"

The bubble followed a downward, opalescent beam of light that glimmered through clouds of haze. Flashing movements of bright color, and strokes of blue and rose, sprinkled with scribbles of silver, cut through the seascape as they continued their descent.

"Oh!" Evie gasped. "This is my dream – this is exactly what I've seen in my dream!"

Lorelei was silent, taking in the reactions of her protégés. Both Evie and Hannah looked awestruck, as indeed, they were. They held hands, their eyes never leaving the sight of the mermaids frolicking beyond the sheer, iridescent wall of the bubble. The mermaids then hitched the bubble by its ribbons to a fleet of passing seahorses. Each mermaid gracefully jumped upon the back of a seahorse, grabbed its intricately jeweled reins, and continued to lead the bubble on its journey.

"Ooh, look," Evie squeaked, marveling at the schools of brilliantly colored fish, in shades of vivid blues and greens, purples and violets, swimming by, crisscrossing each other's path to weave a moving tapestry of colorful circles. The result was also eerily familiar.

"Isn't that ..." Hannah's voice faded.

"... the same pattern as the background of my Mermaid Mahjong Circle painting?" Evie finished for her. "It is!"

Lorelei smiled. "What goes around ..." she said cryptically.

"It's another mermaid connection," Hannah said excitedly. "It's another link in the circle."

The bubble continued its smooth descent as Evie and Hannah stood transfixed, marveling at the sights outside of it. Starfish shimmered, ocean plants glowed like pieces of jade, and bits of coral lent bursts of orange to the seascape.

"I didn't know there was coral growing in the waters around San Francisco," Evie commented.

"Oh, no, we're far from San Francisco now," Lorelei answered with a laugh. "We're thousands upon thousands of miles away – a world away, really – and the things you'll see outside of the bubble are partly real and partly fantasy.

"You're on a path to another reality, a dreamscape if you will," Lorelei continued. "Everything you see exists because someone like you two dreamed it or created it or brought it to life. You're part of a circle that exists because of the women who willed it to life with their creativity. It thrives around you and inside you. And you share it with those who have allowed themselves to lose themselves to their art."

Evie and Hannah just stared at Lorelei. She laughed. "We're almost there," Lorelei continued. "You'll see."

As the bubble continued its descent, Evie and Hannah took it all in, their eyes growing wider by the minute.

At last, the bubble came to rest on a shelf of mother-of-pearl. The mermaids who had been guiding it untied their ribbons and the bubble came to a stop. From nowhere, an unseen door slid open and Lorelei motioned for the two friends to follow her out. They both took in a huge breath and held it. When Lorelei saw their faces, she burst into laughter.

"Oh, no, my dears," she said finally. "You don't need to hold your breath. Just breathe normally." At the looks of puzzlement on their faces, she explained, "The red pouches you're wearing will protect you while you're under the sea."

Evie and Hannah let out their breath in a million bubbles. Then they tentatively took in a new breath and then another.

"Wow," Hannah said, testing her speaking voice underwater. "How cool is this?"

Evie laughed, and her laughter sounded like a tinkling bell.

"Ladies?" Lorelei offered each of them a hand, and the trio got ready to exit the bubble and enter the fairy tale that awaited them.

chapter 41

The moment that Lorelei, Evie, and Hannah stepped outside the crystalline bubble, the transformation happened.

Evie glanced at Lorelei and let out a gasp. The older woman's scarlet-colored dress and shawl had melted away, replaced by a lustrous tail in shades of garnet and ruby. Her long violet-silver hair floated around her like a cloud. Around her neck was a string of tiny seashells, with a mahjong tile charm set in the middle.

"You're breathtaking!" Evie was overcome by Lorelei's presence.

"Oh, my God – look at us!" Hannah exclaimed and Evie turned to her friend.

Hannah's clothing was gone, too, replaced by a shimmering mermaid tail with scales of gold and silver, matching her mane of long, long ringlets. Around her neck she wore the ribbon with the red velvet pouch attached as well as a strand of the tiniest, most perfect diamonds surrounding the mahjong tile charm.

Evie's appearance was equally startling. Her Cal sweatshirt and her jeans had disappeared; in their place was a mermaid tail in shades of peacock blue and deepest emerald that glimmered with the tiniest movement. Her long hair, undone from its usual topknot, swirled around her curves, its color the rich auburn of her youth. She also wore the red pouch on its ribbon around her neck as well as a strand of emeralds with her mermaid mahjong tile at its center.

Dumbfounded, the two women looked at Lorelei for guidance. She laughed merrily and swam off, motioning for them to follow her. Evie pushed off gracefully from the bubble, watching Lorelei for direction in how to flip her tail. In seconds, she was gliding through the water as if she were born to it.

Hannah's start was a bit more problematic. While pushing off she neglected to make sure that she was far enough from the bubble. "Oh, no!" she cried out as, in typical Hannah fashion, the fin of her tail caught on the edge of the bubble's doorway. She tried to swim away with the bubble attached to her.

Evie, by now an expert, swam back. "Easy, Hannah," she said, her tone calm and even. "Here, let me release your fin." With a quick tug, Hannah was freed. "Just watch me for a sec," Evie instructed, demonstrating how to use the mermaid tail. "It's like scuba fins but for the whole bottom half of your body," she said helpfully.

"Spoken by the woman who has always hated the water and never really learned how to swim," Hannah muttered.

"Just relax and let your body move in a fluid motion," Evie tried again.

Hannah glared at her but, in the absurdity of the moment – she was learning to use her mermaid tail? Really? – she began to giggle. And laugh. And guffaw. And at that moment, her body relaxed completely and the mermaid-tail motion came naturally.

"Ooh, this is fun!" she said, swimming along beside Evie. "Who knew?"

Evie shook her head, smiling at Hannah's change in attitude. "Look up ahead!" she said excitedly.

Ahead of them lay what could only be described as a kaleidoscope of mermaids – some perched on pink and lavender shells, brushing their hair with jeweled hairbrushes; some looking into mosaic hand mirrors, admiring their reflections. Others swam in a single loop, creating perfect circles from the tops of their heads to the tips of their tails. Still others played musical instruments – a golden harp, a silvery flute, a violin carved of abalone. More mermaids placed beautifully iced tea cakes out on shell platters.

Evie and Hannah were speechless, not knowing where to look first. Suddenly, Evie grabbed Hannah's hand so tightly that Hannah winced.

"What is it?" she asked her friend.

"That's it, Han," Evie said softly. "That's the inspiration for our mural."

Hannah followed Evie's gaze as she looked out over the realm of mermaids. "Of course, it is," she agreed, her eyes sparkling with excitement. "The mural is everything we see here."

"Created with paint and mosaic and sea glass and jewels …"

"And tapestry and silk and seashells and pastels …"

"And mahjong tiles," they finished together.

"All of that to capture all of this." Evie looked awed, gesturing around her.

"All of that art to capture all of this creative heart," Hannah summed up.

Lorelei appeared at their side in an instant. "Congratulations, girls," she said warmly. "That revelation has just won you a seat at the table over there." She gestured behind her at a small table carved of abalone, surrounded by four seats fashioned of coral. Two of the seats were taken and, upon closer inspection, Evie and Hannah realized that Delia Charlton and Hai Ling – now transformed into mermaids – were seated there.

"Delia?" Evie asked, stunned.

"Actually, it's Cordelia," Delia replied. "That's my real name. Cordelia means 'jewel of the sea.' Delia is just my land name."

"And Hai Ling – is that your real name?" Hannah asked of the second woman.

Hai Ling nodded. "In Chinese, Hai Ling means 'soul of the sea.' My grandmother chose that name for me because she was a mermaid."

Lorelei joined the conversation. "Lorelei is the name of a legendary sea siren whose song, they say, would lure sailors to destruction." She frowned. "All I share with that siren is her name. I love men. I would never harm them." She shook her head definitively.

"And how did you all become mermaids?" Evie asked tentatively. "If you don't mind my asking, that is. Were you born mermaids?"

"Lorelei and I were," Cordelia answered. "As was Hai Ling's grandmother, Meili." Hai Ling nodded. At Evie and Hannah's puzzled looks, she explained. "Meili was the mermaid pictured on the mahjong tiles," she said. "She was my grandmother."

Evie and Hannah's mouths formed perfect o's of amazement.

"My grandmother led me to become a mermaid," Hai Ling explained. "She brought me down under the sea much the same way Lorelei has brought the two of you."

Hannah turned to Lorelei, a question in her eyes.

Lorelei nodded slightly.

"You're going to turn us into mermaids? Forever?"

Lorelei shook her head slightly. "It's not my decision," she told Hannah and Evie. "I'm giving you the opportunity, but the choice is yours."

"What do you mean?" Evie looked shocked.

"Why don't we continue with your adventure right now," Lorelei suggested. "We can talk about whether you want to truly become mermaids once we return to land."

"We're going to talk about whether we want to become mermaids?" Hannah's voice went up several octaves.

"Han, it's okay, don't panic," Evie said. "No one's turning us into mermaids."

"We're going to become mermaids now?" Hannah could not be distracted. "But what about my store? What about the women's art center? What about our lives in San Francisco? What about –"

"Hey, Hannah, take a deep breath," Evie said quietly, putting an arm around her best friend. "It's okay. Nothing is going to change."

Hannah took a couple of deep breaths.

"Better?"

"Better." Hannah smiled. "Sorry, that one kind of blew me away."

"Oh, Hannah, I'm so sorry," Lorelei said. "It seems like I continue to say things that shock either you or Evie. I promised you at the beginning that I mean you no harm at all – I'm just so excited to welcome you to the circle. We're all so happy to finally let you see the fairy-tale world that we've been hinting at. But please, remember that it's all up to you as to whether this experience is just one visit or a complete life change."

"Did she say 'life change' – really?" Hannah was beginning to panic again.

Evie shot Lorelei a pleading look. In response, the older woman nodded. "Nothing has to be decided right now, Hannah," she said soothingly. "In fact, this decision doesn't have any kind of time limit on it."

Evie smiled and Hannah visibly relaxed.

"Right now, though, I think it's time for you both to play a game – a game of mermaid mahjong."

She gestured toward the two empty seats at the table alongside Cordelia and Hai Ling. "Don't worry – we'll teach you how to play," she said, as she seated herself on a nearby rock. "Our game might be a bit different from anything you've seen before, like when you mothers played mahjong," she went on. "We play by mermaid rules."

"Mermaid rules?" Evie laughed.

"How are those different from the regular rules?" Hannah, having calmed down, was curious.

Lorelei laughed. "There are probably just little things here and there," Lorelei said. "For one thing, we don't play with the same number of tiles as you'll find in a full set on land. We only have the one set that Pearl threw overboard, and some of us, as you know, are wearing a tile or two."

Evie and Hannah each reflexively touched the tiles that they wore.

"And, every once in a while, you'll find that a mermaid has taken a few tiles – maybe she's used them to decorate the edge of her hand mirror, or to wear as a hair ornament, or to add to a string of aquamarines around her neck."

"But how can you play mahjong without a full set of tiles?" Evie asked, bewildered.

Lorelei laughed. "All of us mermaids in this circle are artists," she explained. "While our trains of thought might appear illogical to some, our creativity is boundless. Certainly, we might be missing a bam or a krak," she said, alluding to two suits of tiles in the game, "but we can substitute a pink scallop shell or a pearl or a sprig of coral or red algae for anything that we need. Of course, we can also use gold coins, or rubies, or sapphires, or even emeralds."

"Because there's a sunken pirate treasure nearby?" Hannah said weakly.

"Indeed," Lorelei responded. "Clever girl."

"But how do you keep score?" Evie's head was spinning but she was finding herself increasingly enchanted by Lorelei's explanation.

Lorelei let out a tinkling laugh and was joined by Cordelia and Hai Ling. The overall sound effect was one of wind chimes. "Keep score? That's not something we care about," Lorelei said warmly. "As I said, we're all artists here. The joy for us in playing is being able to touch these beautiful, colorful tiles and having the chance to mix the patterns with the colors of the jewels and the textures of the things we love that live in our realm. Everything we see and touch and hear and taste is a way for us to experience art and to make it part of our hearts. Our circle is one of artistic expression. We're not only immersed in the ocean, we're also immersed in the beauty that art provides. And we're committed to continue to create our art forever."

"But how do Evie and I fit in here?" Hannah asked. "I understand that we're both artists and all, but there are so many women who are just as creative as we are. I don't imagine you've met every one of them?"

Lorelei shook her head. "No, of course not." She stopped speaking, looking at something over their shoulders. "Ah, here she comes."

Evie and Hannah spun around, their tails flipping behind them. Approaching was an exquisite mermaid, her tail glowing with topaz and amber, her long hair a rich golden brown. She waved at the mermaids sitting at the mahjong table and hugged Lorelei with a quick, "*Bonjour.*"

"*Chérie, bonjour!*" Lorelei responded as the two mermaids hugged briefly.

"*Alors*, are these them?" the newcomer asked wonderingly.

"*Oui!* Evie, Hannah, may I present Angélique?" she said, making the introduction.

"Angélique?" Now it was Evie's turn to gasp.

"*Bonjour*, Evie, my name on land was actually Angélique Roland."

"You – you're my – you're my –"

"Yes, Angélique is your great-grandmother, Evie," Lorelei explained. "She has been our link to you, the one who made sure that the mahjong tile you found was at that yard sale. She gave it to me to place there in order that you might find it."

"But why?"

"Because I recognized in you the same kind of creative yearning that exists in all of us mermaids," Angélique answered.

"Are you a real mermaid?" Evie asked.

Angélique nodded. "I am."

"I knew it!" Hannah could barely control her excitement. "I knew that you had mermaid blood, Evie."

Evie just stared.

"I understand about why you all feel that Evie should be part of the Mermaid Mahjong Circle, but why me? How did you even know about me?" Hannah asked then.

Lorelei blew out a breath and regarded Hannah closely. "Do you recall your mother playing mahjong?" she asked.

"Of course," Hannah answered.

"And do you recall all of the beautiful clothes and jewelry she had?"

"I do."

Lorelei looked at the other mermaids uneasily. They nodded at her encouragingly. "I'm not sure how to break this to you, Hannah," she said. "But your mother and her circle of mahjong friends – they were all part of this mermaid mahjong circle."

"Are you high?" Hannah's tone was incredulous.

"Try to stay calm, dear," Lorelei soothed.

"I. Am. Calm."

"Hannah, honey, I'm not sure how to tell you this – your mother was a born mermaid."

Hannah started to laugh and then couldn't stop. "My mother – a mermaid!" She doubled over, unable to catch her breath.

Evie, seeing the serious expression on Lorelei's face, went to her friend. "Come on, Hannah," she said softly. "Let's just listen to what Lorelei has to say." She guided Hannah to one of the vacant seats at the mahjong table and then sat down herself in the other one.

"I know it's a shock," Lorelei said apologetically. "I wanted to wait until you and Evie were down here with the rest of us to tell you. I was sure you wouldn't even listen to me if I tried to tell you on land."

Hannah sniffed.

"Hannah, all those beautiful clothes and the jewelry that your mom saved in the attic, all those things that you needed to give away after she died, remember those things?"

"Of course."

"She made those things, Hannah, every single one of them. Every stitch, every jewel setting, every heel and bow on every shoe, every clasp on every purse. Your mother was an amazing artisan and craftsperson."

Hannah looked at Lorelei silently, her eyes never leaving the other woman's face.

"She designed so many of our tails," Lorelei went on.

"Mermaids have a wardrobe of tails?" Evie asked, incredulous.

"Of course," Lorelei answered. "Just because we live underwater most of the time doesn't mean we live under a rock – we love fashion!"

Evie laughed and Hannah, despite herself, did too.

"In fact, I think that the tail I'm wearing today is one of your mom's creations." Lorelei added. "Anyway," she went on, "your mother was born a mermaid a few centuries ago. It was on one of her 'land trips' back in the 1950s that she met your father. He swept her off her feet so completely and she fell so deeply in love that she made the decision never to return to the sea."

Hannah continued to look at Lorelei, her focus unwavering.

"But, as all artists know, you can never really leave your art behind," Lorelei went on. "Even though your mother decided never to return here, she continued to make clothes and jewelry and shoes and bags. She made too much for one person to ever wear, but it was the creating that kept her from missing this," she gestured to their surroundings, "too much."

"So everything we saw at that yard sale – the dresses, the jewelry, all those adorable shoes – those were all Hannah's mother's work?" Evie asked.

Lorelei nodded. "Those were what drew Hannah to my yard," she said.

Hannah finally spoke. "Is my mother here?" she asked haltingly.

Lorelei shook her head sadly. "No, my dear, she's not. You see when she decided to give up her mermaid life for staying on land, she did the one thing that ensured she could never return here. She stopped wearing red."

At Evie and Hannah's questioning looks, she explained. "Once a mermaid visits land, she must always wear something red so that she can return to the sea. Your mother stopped wearing red."

Hannah looked sad. "I thought I might get another chance to see her," she said softly.

Evie hugged her friend. Then a thought struck her. "That's why Aunt Vennie – I mean Pearl – said she always wears something red just in case a last-minute urge to visit here comes over her."

Lorelei nodded. "I think that Pearl's chances of wanting to return here are next to none," she said soberly. She waited a moment and then went on in a happier tone. "So, to answer your question, Hannah, both you and Evie are descendants of mermaids. Combined with your talent for making art out of gems, and Evie's talent as a painter extraordinaire, the two of you are naturals to join us. And, even if you choose to stay on land for the rest of your lives, you will always, always be part of our circle. Your commitment to empowering women through art has won all of our hearts."

"What about my own mother and my grandmother?" Evie asked. "They were both so gifted in the arts – were they mermaids too?"

Angélique shook her head. "It skips generations," she explained. "Not every woman in a mermaid's bloodline becomes a mermaid. While your grandmother and mother – my own blood – were gifted, we chose you because your artistic expressions and your ability to believe are what set you apart."

"And the mahjong tiles?" Evie asked.

"The mahjong tiles are what have brought us together to share our love the arts," Lorelei said.

At this, Hai Ling nodded vigorously. "It wasn't until the tiles trickled down here in a shower of color that we all discovered our mutual passion for the arts," she said.

"And from there, we kind of all 'found' each other." Cordelia continued the tale. "Although I believe that you and Hannah are the last two women we will invite into our realm."

At the looks of surprise on Evie's and Hannah's faces, she explained. "This Mermaid Mahjong Circle has been centuries upon centuries in the making. Pearl's tiles are what brought this group together after lifetimes of being on our own. Then, as the years progressed, we sought to expand our ranks and hoped to discover a few more rare jewels such as yourselves on land, always using the mahjong tiles as a test of whether a woman recognized the beauty she had found and was willing to follow the trail of clues to its conclusion."

"And how many women fit that description?" Hannah asked.

"In all these years … just two."

Evie raised her eyebrow. "You mean …"

Lorelei nodded. "Yes, dear. Only you and Hannah were curious enough, indefatigable enough, patient enough, and passionate enough to follow your hearts for your art."

"So that's it?" Hannah asked. "The circle ends here?"

Cordelia rushed to answer. "The circle of actual mermaids has reached the size it is meant to be," she said gently. "But the circle that you are starting on land with your women's center for the arts – that circle will grow without limit. All thanks to the both of you."

The mermaids applauded Evie and Hannah, who looked excited and awestruck at the same time.

A thought occurred to Hannah. "Lorelei, I have a question," she said. "A few weeks ago you told me that I reminded you so much of someone. Was that my mom?"

Lorelei nodded. "Indeed. You have her same no-nonsense approach to things, her same sense of humor, and, I'm afraid, her same predisposition to knocking things over and having misadventures with your food. It's absolutely adorable."

For the first time since the mermaid revelations, Hannah had a big smile on her face. "Very cool," she said softly.

Angélique leaned in to whisper something into Lorelei's ear. "Of course, of course," Lorelei responded. "How could I forget that? Evie and Hannah, are you ready to try your hand at Mermaid Mahjong?"

The two friends nodded eagerly, listening as Angélique and Hai Ling explained the game and their rules.

"Don't worry," Lorelei said, laughing at the confusion on their faces. "I'll play alongside you to guide you along. But first," she paused dramatically. "First it's time for you each to reach into the red pouch around your neck and pull out the dice inside."

Evie and Hannah each removed their dice, and handed them to Lorelei.

"It's traditional to start a game of mahjong with each of the four players rolling the dice. The player who rolls the highest number assumes the role of East, meaning that she goes first in play," Lorelei told them. "So by using the dice that the two of you have brought, you are officially welcomed to your very first Mermaid Mahjong game. Go ahead, Evie, throw the dice."

Evie threw, followed by Hannah, Hai Ling, and Angélique. To no one's surprise, Evie's roll was the highest and she was named East. And from there, Lorelei led the friends through the rounds of picking tiles, sorting out bams from kraks (from the occasional scallop shell or emerald or gold coin) and creating their very first mahjong hands.

chapter 42

The sun was just breaking over the horizon when Evie woke. She raised her head slowly, trying to remember why it was that she was on Baker Beach. And why Hannah was slowly waking up a few feet away. Standing up carefully, she brushed damp sand off the sleeve of her Cal sweatshirt and from her jeans. She still wore the red velvet pouch on a ribbon around her neck. Hannah, she noticed, did as well.

"What are we still doing here?" Hannah asked, her voice raspy from sleep. "The last thing I remember is that we met Lorelei here last night … then there was some kind of windstorm and then …?" Her voice trailed off questioningly.

"I'm not sure," Evie answered slowly. "I'm still trying to wake up from this wild dream I had about us being underwater with Lorelei and these other mermaids."

Hannah turned pale. "Me too!" she exclaimed. "And we traveled down there in this enormous bubble pulled by mermaids …"

"Holding red ribbons and riding seahorses."

"And I found out that my mother was a mermaid."

"And I met my great-grandmother."

"And we played Mermaid Mahjong!" This last piece was said in unison as the two women looked at each other in amazement.

As Evie shook her head to clear it, she noticed a pink-tinged seashell a few feet away with something flapping under it. Leaning down, she picked up the shell and the water-stained piece of parchment. Then, she read it aloud:

Dearest Evie & Hannah
Your dreams were real, your hearts are true
The mermaids will forever call to you.
Your life with us beneath the sea
Is always a possibility
As long as the color red you wear –
keep the pouch and ribbon always near.
You'll see us perhaps once in a while
In your dreams or maybe a grocery aisle.
We encircle you with beams of love and light,
With gleaming tones and colors bright.
Remember that your mural creation
Will be the source of much inspiration
For women to flower, to tower, to empower.
This is your time, your legacy, your hour.
Love, Lorelei, Angélique, Hai Ling & Cordelia
& All the Mermaid Mahjong Circle

chapter 43

Three Years Later

The September afternoon sun cast its brilliant autumn light on the trees bordering the entrance of the new women's arts center, bringing a painterly feeling to the setting. A sign in brushed copper calligraphy announced *The Mermaid Mahjong Circle: A Women's Center for the Arts.* Women from all walks of life – painters, writers, sculptors, musicians, singers, actors – passed through the doorway proudly, excited to have a forum to support their artistic goals. Admission was free, with donations suggested, so that any woman who wanted to could come in to be inspired.

Evie and Hannah stood by the entrance, greeting visitors as they arrived. Evie's hair was wound into an updo and held in place by a pair of red lacquer chopsticks. Hannah's red carnelian earrings dangled from her ears.

"I can't believe this day is finally here," Evie said to Hannah softly. "It's all come together so beautifully!"

Hannah nodded enthusiastically, her silvery-gold curls bobbing. "It was a labor of love," she agreed warmly.

Over the past two years, the two friends had worked hard to put together a team of women to help them create the center. Word of mouth – starting with Hannah's jewelry-store customers and her suppliers, as well as Evie's gallery contacts and their connections, and including a crackerjack social media effort spearheaded by Hannah's niece, Emma – built a groundswell of interest in the center. Generous contributions by many of the city's fine-arts patrons – including a certain Mrs. Vennie Harper – were added to Hannah's financial backing to make the Center a reality. Emma's efforts extended to the city's vast network of schools – from middle schools to high schools to colleges and universities – creating a huge sense of awareness for the women's arts center and generating tremendous interest among young women in the arts.

"It's never too early to feed a passion in the arts or to bring out the hidden artist within," Vennie commented when Evie and Hannah had told her about their progress.

"You're right, Aunt Vennie," Evie said, giving her a hug. "Hannah and I were lucky to have our artistic interests noticed and supported early on by our parents. Hopefully, the Center will give those same kinds of opportunities to all young women and girls who want them."

Evie and Hannah's joy on their big day was tinged with some sadness – they had lost Aunt Vennie just a year before the center was completed. But a scholarship in her name – the Pearl Venus Harper Circle Grant – would ensure that her spirit would live on in the works of several deserving young artists each year.

At exactly two o'clock, the opening festivities began. Evie and Hannah stood at one end of the art center's lobby, with two hundred or so guests standing before them. Behind them on the wall was a huge panel draped in aquamarine silk, waiting to be unveiled.

"We want to thank you all for being here today," Hannah began, "to help us open The Mermaid Mahjong Circle: A Women's Center for the Arts."

Applause sounded throughout the room.

"The story behind this center is unusual, to say the least, as is the name," Evie joined in. "In fact, I'm not sure you would believe it if we told it to you." She smiled.

The crowd, thinking she was joking, laughed.

"Let's just say it involves some very determined mermaids and some very unusual mahjong tiles," Hannah added. She and Evie exchanged a quick look as the audience laughed again.

"But seriously," Evie went on, "this center was created because Hannah and I both feel so strongly that, for those women who believe, as we do, that their art and their heart are one and the same, there should be a place that supports and nurtures those artistic talents. A place that teaches. A place that allows them to share their art with others."

"The Mermaid Mahjong Circle Center is that place," Hannah continued. "It was created by women for women. It's where you can visit to see exhibits and performances of all kinds. It's where you can take classes in an entire range of artistic pursuits – music, painting, writing, weaving, cooking, and on and on. And it's a place to share your expertise with others. A place to feel empowered by your art."

She paused for a moment and touched the mahjong tile necklace at her throat. "We believe that art, like life, is a circle," she said. "Art inspires art – it is a legacy that is passed down from one point in time to another, often along invisible or unexpected paths." She smiled at her audience. "Evie and I were inspired to create this arts center because we want to keep that circle whole and unbroken."

Her eyes welled up.

Evie reached over and took Hannah's hand, squeezing it in understanding. "Creating this center has really been a work of art and a labor of love for us," she said. "And we hope that it motivates all of you to live your art, to immerse yourself in it as completely as you can, and to let it take you to a world you may never have imagined."

Murmurs of appreciation ran through the audience.

"And now, it's time to see what all the fuss is about," Evie said, her tone less serious. "We've put together a brochure with all the details," she went on, pointing to a table piled high with the booklets, "so please take one for yourself and for a friend. And please remember, as we are just getting started, that like any piece of art, this center is a work in progress."

An appreciative chuckle ran through the audience.

"Before we send you all off to explore all that the center can offer – and to see how very cool this place is – I think it's time to reveal our artistic centerpiece," Hannah said, indicating the draped panel behind them.

Evie nodded in agreement. "This piece tells the story of the Mermaid Mahjong Circle Center," she explained. "And while it may look like a fairy tale or a fantasy to you, well…" Here she paused, her gaze traveling over the audience. A startled look crossed her face, but she recovered quickly. Three familiar faces in the throng smiled back at her. Lorelei, Hai Ling, and Delia were standing in the midst of the audience, smiling proudly at Evie and Hannah. Evie went back to her remarks. "Well, in fact, it is. A fairy tale that has actually come true."

She and Hannah stepped over to the wall hanging and, a moment later, the two women carefully released the cloth that had been covering it. The cloth fell to the ground with a whoosh and the audience stood there, speechless.

The Mermaid Mahjong Circle was revealed.

chapter 44

The room was silent. Then the applause started slowly and increased in volume until neither Evie nor Hannah could hear themselves saying, "Thank you. Thank you everyone!" Cameras starting flashing and the friends joined hands and raised them over their heads.

"Beautiful!" "Amazing!" "I've never seen anything like it!" "Are those real jewels?" "Are those mermaids?" "How did you ever think of it?" "What was your inspiration?"

The comments and questions flew. The audience was clearly smitten – the Mermaid Mahjong Circle mural went viral in moments.

The mural was nothing short of mesmerizing. It took up nearly an entire wall, was circular in shape, and depicted Evie and Hannah's adventure under the sea. Made up of multiple panels, each done in a different art form, the mural captured the mermaids in all their joyful artistry, with the table of mermaids playing mahjong at the center.

Most wondrous about the mural was that it was a collage of different kinds of art, all created by Evie and

Hannah. Some of the panels were painted in watercolor, some in oils; others were done in a mosaic of sea glass or hand-painted tiles. Portions were crafted from weaving and embroidery, while others were embedded with jewels. Evie's original concept for the pattern of circles of color, mimicking the scales on the mermaids' tails, was carried throughout the mural, varying in shades from deepest indigo to rich turquoise to cornflower blue and celadon green. Also evoked throughout the mural was the theme of the mahjong tiles, which Hannah had rendered out of stained glass and placed throughout the piece. Sea creatures created out of jewels swam among mermaids with tails of hammered gold and silver. Seashells woven in pastel shades of silk were embellished with pearls in shades from white to cream to pink to ebony.

Taken separately, each panel of the mural evoked one moment of Evie and Hannah's mermaid adventure. Taken in its entirety, however, the mural was a powerful and poignant tribute to the art and the heart of a woman.

It was a tremendous undertaking, one which everyone at the event assumed had been created completely by Evie and Hannah. And it had been. Almost. What the two women did not reveal to their audience was that they had had some help. It seemed that whenever they returned to their work after several hours away from it, they found that another little piece of the mural had been worked on. Evie and Hannah were certain that their fairy godmermaids had had a hand in providing some finishing touches.

epilogue

The cold, damp sand was firm under their feet as Evie and Hannah strolled along the water's edge at Baker Beach. The sun had barely risen that December morning as two friends took their now-weekly Saturday morning stroll, chatting about the past week's goings-on at the Mermaid Mahjong Circle arts center. The women were bundled up in sweats and puffy parkas against the chill in the air – Evie all in black and Hannah in shades of cream and off-white.

The only spark of color in what either woman was wearing was the red velvet pouch holding the mahjong dice, which each of them carried in their pocket.

After a few minutes, Evie stopped walking. Hannah, caught up in describing the latest piece that she was designing for the Ocean's Enchantment Collection, kept on walking a few feet more before she realized that Evie was no longer with her.

"Sorry," she said with a silly grin. "I guess I got caught up in my story."

Evie smiled. Hannah was being Hannah.

"Wait," Hannah said, realization dawning on her face. "Is this the spot?"

"It is."

"Are you sure?"

Evie spoke softly. "As sure as I am that we're part of the Mermaid Mahjong Circle."

"And are you sure about our decision?"

Evie nodded. "I am."

Now it was Hannah's turn to nod. "Me too," she said. "I guess it's time, then."

The two women reached into their pockets and pulled out the red pouches holding the ruby dice. They looked at each other for a moment and then, in one tandem gesture, threw their pouches back into the sea. The pouches floated for a moment and then disappeared from sight.

Evie and Hannah stood at the shoreline for a moment, each lost in her own thoughts. Then they hugged, in a circle of warmth, of friendship, and of love. Arm in arm, they walked away, back to their lives and all the art that was yet to be created.

Evie slipped her hand into her pocket to pull out her car keys and then stopped still. Her fingers closed around something else – the red velvet pouch with the ruby dice – somehow magically returned there. She shook her head and smiled.

In the distance there was the sound of tinkling laughter.

the end

Made in the USA
Columbia, SC
08 October 2020

22401572R00119